Beyond Gray Skies

By 

Danielle Sibarium

Dedication

My friends and colleagues of the Jackson Writer's Group.

Most especially Karen Kelly Boyce, JJ Lair, Al Lohn, Louise Ann Barton, Chris Iavarone, Pete Postorino, Barbara Hosbach, Nicole Labrocca, Donna Rose, Beth Rinu, Alison Deluca, Pat Pattan and Patrick LaMorte and everyone else I met at this incredible group of writers through the years.

You have all in some way welcomed me, influenced me, supported me, and taught me how to look at my own work with a more critical eye. You have helped me through days of writer's block, fear of speaking in front of groups, and book signings I feared no one would show up to. Thank you!

Chapter 1

I work to catch my breath. The sobs come fast and hard. My nose is clogged and I can't breathe. My chest hurts. Aches. I take a shallow breath. Then another. It takes a minute but as I gift my lungs with air I settle down.

I almost wish I didn't. I'm empty. Broken. Destroyed.

The crying stopped but a fresh wave of tears streams down my cheeks. *How much longer can I go on like this?* Faking it, going through the motions? I take another long look into his blue eyes. No matter how hard I search them, they're flat. Devoid of what I'm looking for.

A spark. Recognition. Life.

I miss the way his face lit up when he looked at me. The playful twinkle in his eyes when we spotted each other across a crowded room.

I clutch the framed picture to my chest wishing it was him, warm and in the flesh instead of just a moment in time, an image captured and encapsulated in cold, hard glass. What

I wouldn't give for one more touch. One more kiss. One more chance to say I love you.

Missing him hurts. The pain slices through every cell of my body. It destroys me. Everything I do, everywhere I look, reminders of him tease and torment me. Memories bombard and overwhelm me.

I glance at the oven clock. Shit. Dinner's late. I'm making Keith's favorite, roasted chicken, scalloped potatoes and brussel sprouts. It's a simple meal, but my husband loves it. He's been so attentive lately, sneaking in sexy time when we can and helping around the house. I want him to know how much I appreciate it.

I thought I had all the ingredients, but as I started prepping I remembered I used all the lemons. It's no big deal, nothing a quick run to the supermarket couldn't fix. I just didn't expect to hit so much traffic on the way home.

Something's going on in town. Police barricades closed streets off and sirens rang out loud and ugly. Emergency vehicles raced by me. When I have a minute, I'll hop on social media and see what's going on. Maybe Keith knows. He took the day off, and after spending a morning together in bed, he ran errands for me.

Keith dropped by the library to return some books, picked clothes up from the dry cleaners and ran to the post office for stamps. Come to think of it, he should've been home by now. The craziness in town seems to have delayed him, too. If I'm lucky I'll finish cooking dinner before he gets home.

The ringing doorbell startles me I drop the spoon in my hand on the floor. The clanking of metal on the tile echoes through the room. Bumps cover my skin. For some reason the bell chime sounds five times louder than normal. My arms cover in goose flesh.

It's a rare moment when my eleven year old isn't raising hell. He's not blasting his music. Doesn't have the television or gaming system turned up to deafening levels. Everything feels off kilter, starting with the bell breaking the unnatural silence around me.

My breath catches in my throat at the sight of the two officers on the other side of the door.

"Mrs, Collins?" The taller officer asks.

No! No, no, no! I want to slam the door in their faces. If I don't let them speak it isn't real. I've seen this on television and in movies. I've read about it. No way! NO!

Neither man looks comfortable, or happy. Both officers remove their hats from their heads.

"May we come inside."

NO! My brain screams. I shake my head back and forth. I don't want them on my porch or in my house. I want to run and hide.

"Mom," Logan calls, coming to stand beside me. "What's going on?"

Tears fill my eyes as a thickness forms in the back of my throat. I open my mouth to speak, but I can't. I can't breathe. I need to hold it together and stay strong for my son. I don't know if I can with my legs turning to rubber.

"Mom!" Logan's scared voice rises an octave or ten. "What's wrong, why are they here?"

I close my eyes, take a deep breath and roll my shoulders back. I need to let the cops in, and listen to what they have to say. It happens in slow motion, as if I'm watching the scene from somewhere else in the room.

My brain can't process their words. My heart is about to explode. My lungs don't want to take in air. I pull my son in my arms. I clutch him to my chest. Hold on to him tight. Tears stream down Logan's face and he sobs with his whole body, I know I need to find my way forward for him. Today. Tomorrow. Indefinitely.

Two years have passed, but it isn't any easier. The pain is fresh. Sharp. His loss devastates me as much today as it did when I first found out Keith had been crushed by a car that crashed into the dry cleaners.

A previously convicted drunk driver lost control of his car when he turned into the strip mall. In an attempt to avoid pedestrians, he accidentally hit the gas and turned the wheel hard, crashing through the storefront and right over my husband.

"Mom," Logan calls from the other side of my bedroom door. "Are you okay?"

I sniffle and try to pull myself together. The key word is try.

"Yes, sweetheart. Just tired."

I hate lying to him, but he's taken his father's death so hard, I don't want to stir up any pain.

"Can I come in?"

"Um." I clear my throat, blow my nose and wipe my eyes. "Sure."

The door creaks open. My son doesn't move. He stands at the entrance to my bedroom, and evaluates me.

"You're not tired, you've been crying."

"I'm fine, Logan. Really. I'm just a little emotional."

He nods as he approaches the bed and sits at the edge.

"I'm going to find a way to kill that fucker."

"Logan! Your language!" I scold.

"Fuck my language. That asshole should've been in jail. Instead he was out on the streets, doing exactly what he was arrested for in the first place. Only this time he killed my father. When I'm old enough I'm going to hunt him down and destroy him and his family."

Maybe I should be grateful that my son wants to avenge his father's wrongful death. Maybe it will motivate him to do something great with his future. Perhaps he'll want to become a doctor to deal with addiction and save lives. Or a lawyer to prosecute criminals. I *should* be proud.

I'm not. I'm terrified. I'm scared to death of him doing something out of anger and then I'll lose him, too.

"Sweetheart, I know you miss your father. I do too. But he wouldn't want you to sacrifice all the good things you have yet to come in your life for revenge. He'd want you to become all you can be."

"Dad taught me to stand up for what's right. He said I should never be afraid as long as I'm on the right side of the issue."

I nod. "Yes. But you're talking about destroying potentially innocent people. There's nothing right about that."

"There is, if it saves lives. If he has a family they might all be like him."

Logan says it so matter of fact and emotionless. His words send shivers down my spine. I understand my son's position. I'd like nothing more than to run my car over the bastard that stole my husband and crush him the way he crushed Keith, but I can't. Logan is the only thing that keeps me from doing something dumb and makes life bearable. I have to trust in the system.

"He's behind bars. He's not coming out this time. Let him rot there like the piece of garbage he is."

"That isn't enough. I want him to suffer. We do. Besides, you don't know how long he'll be in there or if he'll get paroled. And then what? Huh? Dad will still be dead and he'll be able to live. To have a life like nothing happened because alcoholism is a disease. "

Logan doesn't talk much about his feelings. He doesn't show that the pain of losing his father is like an open chest wound. Wearing emotions on the sleeve, that's my specialty, and I see firsthand the effect it's having on my son.

"Get over here."

I sit back, lean against the headboard, and stretch my arms open for my son.

He shakes his head. "I'm not a baby, Mom. A hug isn't going to fix what's wrong with me."

Not what I needed to hear right now. He's right. He's not a baby. But he'll always be *my* baby. I'll always want to mother him. Love him. Protect him. Hugs are just a natural consequence of those other things.

Chapter 2

"The reason I'm calling, Mrs. Collins," the man on the other end of the line explains. "Is that Logan threatened to cut a boys penis off at lunch today."

"Logan wouldn't just say something like that. I'm sure the other boy did something to prompt my son."

"This isn't the first time something like this has happened."

"You're right. And the last time he threatened someone, a kid opened five packs of ketchup and squeezed them out all over Logan's head."

"Regardless, we have a zero tolerance policy and I was able to justify not punishing Logan last time because someone did something to his person, and your son didn't retaliate in any physical manner. This time, however, I have a lunch table full of boys that heard Logan's unprompted threat. Perhaps it's time to seek help."

"What?"

"I think we should stop pussyfooting around the fact that your son is a bomb ready to explode. He's very angry. It's time Logan sees a psychiatrist. We have a list of doctors the district uses if you'd like recommendations."

"Maybe what he needs is a little more positive attention and understanding at school, Mr. Butler."

I recognize the frustration in the long sigh coming over the phone. "This is an official warning. If Logan doesn't straighten his act out I'm going to have to get the authorities involved. I can't follow the old adage of let boys be boys and look the other way. Not in today's environment."

"I'm not asking you to look the other way. I'm asking for fairness and a little bit of understanding."

"Here at Roosevelt Middle School, we pride ourselves on treating all of our students with fairness and understanding. It would serve you well to remember that."

I'm not sure but I think that jerk of an assistant principal made some sort of threat. He's had it out for my son since his first year at the school. He's made comments about how boys without fathers tend to be rambunctious troublemakers.

"In my opinion, you've been too understanding. Too permissive when it comes to your son's aggressive behavior."

"That's not your call to make."

"Perhaps, if he had a strong male role model around to teach him how to deal with his violent tendencies . . ."

I bite my tongue and tune the moron out. Maybe the asshole thinks I should've married the first warm body I bumped into after I lowered my husband into the ground.

Too bad this conversation isn't taped. The superintendent needs to hear this first hand. I can write a long letter to him and the entire board detailing how this man has mishandled my son from the day he walked into that school.

Even if I do and he gets reprimanded, he'll turn it around and claim that I misinterpreted his statement. Along with all the bullshit he's thrown my way. He'll pull the man card and say I'm over-sensitive because I'm letting my emotions get in the way of reason.

As if he'd ever recognize reason. He wouldn't know it if it slapped him in the face. That's why there's a conglomerate of parents working actively to have him removed. The sooner the better.

*

I look at the clock on my dashboard. It's a quarter to five. Logan should've been out of practice fifteen minutes ago. Mine is one of the last cars in the parking lot. I don't want to smother him and be one of those helicopter mom's, but I'm concerned.

I check my phone for a missed message, but there isn't one. I don't know what's going on and the last thing I need is for him to get into some sort of trouble. Not after the call I got earlier in the day.

I leave my car and start up the steps leading into the school. Laser focused, I don't pay any attention to the man coming out of the building.

"May I help you?" He stops to ask.

I barely give the man in sweats and a t-shirt a cursory glance as I answer. "I need to see Mr. Archer."

"Can you tell me what this is in reference to?"

I don't want to get into this, but I know those damn doors are locked and I need to get in. With my eyes on the entrance, hoping the door will open, I offer a vague answer.

"He's the volleyball coach and my son hasn't come out of practice yet. I want to make sure everything's okay and that there aren't any problems."

"There aren't," he says in a tone that's too light and airy for me to take seriously.

Condescending jerk. I don't have time for games or mindless chit chat. I need to find my son ASAP. I take a deep breath, so I can explain that I need in there and time is of the essence.

Standing strong and tall I meet his eyes. Bright blue eyes with swirls of gray stare back at me. Vibrant eyes full of life. Eyes so intense they pull me close and hold me still.

I feel exposed. Like he peeled back my skin and peeked inside me, behind the facade I keep in place for the world to see. I search for words, but they're lost. Forgotten. I drop my eyes to reset.

I never had a reaction like this before, to anyone. It throws me for a loop. I didn't expect this. Now I know better. I won't be taken in by his looks and rocked to my core. I gather my strength determined to do this right.

Only I don't.

My eyes open and find his still locked on me. Staring at me. Soaking me in like nothing else exists. My heart races as I stare into two warm pools of blue that I want to drown in. Air leaves my lungs in a hurry. He knocked the wind out of me. I stand captivated by those eyes, unable to do anything but stare at him and his perfectly sculpted features.

Aside from the eyes that can be mistaken for gemstones, his jaw is strong. Solid. And his nose turns up just a bit at the end. All of this perfection is framed by dirty blonde hair with lighter streaks on the top. The front of his too long hair hangs below his eyebrows and just above his lashes. It's not so long that it hides his face, just long enough for me to want to run my hand through it to brush it back and get a better view of his playful eyes.

As if he knows the reaction he's having on me, his full, pillowy lips curl into a smile. The type of smile you see on commercials for breath mints or mouthwash. Fresh and clean with straight white teeth. The type of mouth you want to meet with your own to feel the tingle of his warm peppermint breath.

I don't know how much time passes while I'm held captive by his eyes. I'm lightheaded from a lack of oxygen. I need to turn this around. I force myself to pull in a deep breath before the light dims and I fall at this man's feet.

It's more than his smile that melts me like chocolate in the sun. It's not his kind but mischievous eyes either. It's him. The whole damn package including the kind, concerned look on his face that makes me want to stay and talk to this beautiful stranger.

Where the hell did this come from?

I don't understand this reaction. It's foreign. Like my mind short circuited. It's faltering like an overused battery, unable to turn over. I close my eyes and shake off thoughts about this man and refocus them where they belong. On my son. On Logan.

"I'm Mason Archer." The man offers his hand to me.

Mason Archer. What a perfect name. It's unique and strong. Majestic. Like his effect on me. *I'm really losing it.*

"You? But you're so young."

I'm mortified by the tone of my voice, as if being young is something offensive.

He smiles again. A perfect smile. His blue eyes reach into my soul and knead the pain and darkness there. It's being massaged. Manipulated. It hurts, but the pain is what reminds me that I'm still alive.

My heart rate picks up speed. I don't want to look away from him. I avoid it as long as I can, wondering if my hair is a mess, and cursing myself for not putting make-up on before I left the house.

I'm flustered and angry at myself. Why? Why is this man, this man that's so young I'm not sure he's legal, having this kind of effect on me?

"I'm going to pretend you meant that as a compliment," he says stroking his thumb across his bottom lip. Bringing my focus to his pouty lips once again. "Even though the look on your face says you're troubled."

"No. Of course not." I compose myself and regain some semblance of the woman I am. The woman I was before this conversation started. "I just thought the coach . . . I mean you . . . were one of the teachers in the school. I just expected him . . . you . . . to look different."

"Different how?" His head tilts, his brows furrow as he contemplates me or what I'm saying. I'm not sure which. I think he's even more attractive wearing this serious face than he was a moment ago flashing his dazzling smile.

Attractive? Shit where did that come from?

"Older. Not as physically fit." Why can't I shut my mouth? I wish the ground would swallow me up.

"Ah, fat and out of shape." He laughs. His tongue peeks out of his mouth and wets his bottom lip before a smirk covers his face. "Well, I am a teacher here, and I can't say

I'm upset I've left you with a better impression than the one you imagined." His eyes shine playfully as he looks me over. Why is he looking at me with hunger in his eyes? Suddenly I'm insecure about my ripped jeans and the old, washed out, possibly stained, shirt I'm wearing. "I don't like when things are one sided."

Is he flirting? He can't flirt with me, aside from the age difference between us, he's my son's coach, and I'm a married woman. That last thought cuts off my breath and threatens to choke me. It rips into my heart like a samurai sword. Sharp. Cold. Deadly.

I'm not married. Not anymore. I'm a widow and have been every day for the past two years.

"Mom! What are you doing?" Logan shouts.

My eyes find my son exiting the building. Guilt overwhelms me. My eyes fall to the ground as I scramble to find words to explain my actions. I can't tell my son that at this very moment, I'm having unsavory thoughts about his hot coach.

"Hey, Logan, cut your mother some slack," Mr. Archer comes to my defense. "You're late and she's worried about you. You left the gym over ten minutes ago. What took so long?"

"Nothing." My son looks away. He's lying.

"I can't help if you don't tell me what's going on."

"Mr. Johnson stopped me on the way out. He wanted to talk for a minute. Turns out his idea of a minute is everyone else's idea of ten minutes."

"Isn't Mr. Johnson the school psychologist?" I ask.

"Mom! I don't want to talk about this!"

"Hey, now." Mr. Archer starts, with his hand on Logan's shoulder. "That's no way to talk to your mother. She's just doing her job."

I'm choked up listening to the way this too-young-to-be-a-teacher-man diffuse Logan's anger. It reminds me of Keith. My heart shrieks at the thought. Whenever Logan gave me a hard time, his father would get involved and turn the flame down on both ends of the fire.

"Sorry, Mom." I know he doesn't mean it. He's saying it because Mr. Archer told him to, but it is an apology. Sincere or not, I'll take it. For now.

"That's better. Now, did you tell him what that boy said to you?"

Staring at the ground Logan draws a line in the cement with his toes. "No."

"What did he say?" I jump in. I knew it! I knew Logan was provoked.

"I'm not talking about this."

"It's okay Logan. You can tell you're mother." Obviously Mr. Archer knows something I don't.

"No. All I need is for you to teach me how to fight. I mean really fight. Then I can kick his a—"

"Logan!" There is a stern warning in Mr. Archer's tone.

My son looks up at this man who holds influence over him and complies, even though his eyes rage with anger. He takes a long, deep breath before speaking.

"I didn't start this. Why am I the only one who's getting in trouble?"

"Can someone tell me what the hell is going on?" Frustration sounds in my voice.

"Please don't," Logan implores, his eyes wide and pleading.

I'll be honest. The fact that my son has entrusted a complete and total stranger while shutting me out hurts. It eats away at me like vultures picking at a dead carcass. He's the only thing that keeps me holding on most days, and he clearly doesn't want me involved in this part of his life. In any part of his life lately. I'm beside myself. No. I'm outright pissed at both of them.

"Someone needs to fill me in!" I shriek.

I sound like a shrew. I bet Mr. Archer thinks this is why Logan doesn't want to tell me. He probably doesn't blame my son. At this point, I'm not sure I do.

"Let's take this down to the parking lot." Mr. Archer nudges his head forward after glancing behind us.

"This whole thing is bullshit!" Logan practically shouts as we walk toward our car. "I didn't do anything! They started."

"Why don't you get in while I talk to your mother for a minute."

"What? No!"

"Logan, I'm not asking you! Get in the car or you're benched for our first meet."

The breath leaves my son fast and furious like a punctured balloon.

I press a button on the key fob to unlock the car. With a loud huff and a slam of the door, Logan leaves us alone to speak.

"I'm sorry," I say, looking at my sulking son in the car. "I don't know what has him so up in arms right now. He's usually not so rude and disrespectful."

"I understand." Mr. Archer assures me. But, still I feel the need to explain Logan's behavior. Only I can't. Because he doesn't talk to me and no one will tell me what's really going on.

"Has Logan mentioned anything about his friend Delaney?"

I shake my head. "No. This is about a girl? I can't believe him!"

"You might feel different when you hear the whole story."

I stop my tirade. Blow out a frustrated breath and listen as Mr. Archer explains.

"Delaney's father just died."

"Oh no." I cover my mouth afraid to hear where this is going next.

Tears fill my eyes. It's an automatic response. I hear something sad and heartbreaking, I cry. A baby is born, I cry. The wind blows, I cry. No matter what life throws at me, my response over the last two years is to cry.

"He was a police officer and it seems he was ambushed. Goaded into a foot chase then shot by a group of gang members waiting for him."

"That poor girl."

I squeeze my eyes closed fighting to hold back the tears, determined not to look unstable. Now it makes sense why Logan fought so hard to keep me in the dark. He didn't want my mind to race back to Keith like it just did. Like it always does.

"Logan's been trying to help her through this difficult time." *Of course he would.* " Turns out, there's a boy in our school whose father was recently arrested a few towns over for sexual assault. I can't tell you his name, but the boy claims her father arrested his father, and the murder was retribution."

"I'm sorry, I still don't understand what this has to do with my son." I wipe away the disobedient tears that fall from my eyes.

"Are you all right?" Mr. Archer asks, placing his hand on my shoulder.

I nod, wishing he didn't touch me because this little gesture of comfort is one that I haven't had in forever and I welcome it.

It's physical contact with someone other than my son. It's nice. And sweet. And just one more reminder that I have no one, no source of comfort waiting for me back at home.

The problem is I like the warmth of his hand on me. It sends a radiating heat down my arm and through the rest of my body. For the first time since Keith died that bone chilling cold running through my veins has dissipated.

I want more of this. More warmth and touching. More concern and comfort showered on me. I'll even go so far as to say I want a hug. A strong, tight hug meant to shield and protect me from the world. Someone's arms to hold me for a minute or an hour. What I want most of all is a real, solid, literal shoulder to cry on.

What the hell is wrong with me? I lost it. Lost what's left of my mind. I'm stronger than this. I've had to be and I don't melt because a guy is good looking and noticed me. I squeeze my eyes closed for a beat, clear my head, and pull myself together. I have to. For Logan.

"I'm sorry," I sniffle, and clear my throat. "I'm fine. I just . . . I'm fine."

As if he knows he is what set me off, Mr. Archer removes his hand, stuffs it in his pocket, and continues. "The boy and a few of his friends sat with Logan and Delaney at lunch today. According to the girl and your son, the other boy threatened to follow her home and rape her. That's when Logan threatened to cut the boy's penis off."

"And they were surrounded by the boy's friends which is why there's a table full of witnesses."

He nods. "Yes. I'm pretty sure they set Logan up to neutralize him. This way if anything happens, Logan is the one that gets in trouble."

"Didn't anyone else hear? Did the girl corroborate Logan's version of the story?" I ask running my hand through my hair.

"She did. Unfortunately she's the only one. The boys all said she made it up because she's looking for attention. I guess someone believes it's plausible due to recent events."

"Not someone, Mr. Butler."

"Unfortunately."

"But if this kid's father was arrested, shouldn't Logan get the benefit of the doubt?"

"It's not my call to make."

"You don't believe my son either."

I'm not asking him, I'm declaring it. And the very fact that I'm saying these words leaves me with the bitter taste of betrayal on my lips. I don't understand why this strikes so deep. I shouldn't care what anyone thinks. I believe my son and that's enough for me. After all, it's him and me against the world.

"I didn't say that. What I believe and what I can prove are two very different things. I'm trying to give Logan an outlet and an ear to work through some of these things. I shouldn't have given you as much information as I did, but I think Logan did what he believed was right, even if the outcome wasn't the desired one."

I shake my head determined not to allow another tear to fall. "I'm proud of him. He tried to do the right thing."

"He did. But he needs to steer clear of this other boy for the time being. At least until Mr. Johnson's investigation is complete."

"Investigation?"

Mr. Archer nods, and I can tell by the annoyed look on his face he thinks this is bullshit, too.

"The school has to take the threat seriously, so Mr. Butler referred it to Mr. Johnson."

"What about the threat to that poor girl? Are they investigating that, too?"

Mr. Archer's face takes on a hard, stoic look. His eyes trail off over to something in the distance. His non-answer is all I need.

"Let's work on keeping Logan focused and off the radar. I think that's the best shot of keeping him in the clear. I explained it all, but I'm not sure I got through to him. So it would help if you could reiterate the message."

"So we're clear, what do you want him to do if something else happens? If it escalates?"

"Let's not think about that just yet."

"Please, Mr. Archer, I need to know. What will happen to my son?"

"Depends on what happens and what witnesses report."

"So if this punk is in a group of his friends and they surround my son and beat the shit out of him, Logan could still be the one to take the fall?"

Mr. Archer looks at me long and hard before answering. "I'm doing my best to make sure that doesn't happen."

*

The ten minute ride home from school is spent in silence. Not exactly silence. I hear the buzzing of my son's phone notifying him of new messages. They come in non-stop. Before he finishes typing a response, two or three alerts come at him.

"Who are you talking to?"

"I'm not talking,"

"Fine. Who are you texting with?"

"It's snap," he answers annoyed. "No one special. Some kids from school."

"The boys that are causing the problems?"

"No, Mom. Geez, stay out of it."

"I can't. I'm your mother and I'm worried about you."

"Don't be. I got this."

That's it. The last thing my son says to me on the ride, through dinner and for the rest of the night. He shut down and he's freezing me out. I'm so stressed over the whole situation. And angry. Angry at the school, at Mr. Butler, and angry at my son.

How I wish I had something besides a bottle of wine to warm me up and keep me company.

Chapter 3

I wipe under my eyes with my fingers, removing any excess eyeliner that's not where it's supposed to be. I check my makeup one more time in the rearview mirror before getting out of the car. Make-up's neat. Hair's in place. I'm good to go.

I walk to the middle school at a brisk pace. I hope the match didn't start yet. *I'm only here to support my son,* I repeat over and over on the walk into the gym. I am. This seems to be the only way Logan and I can connect. He's pretty much shut me out of everything else in his life. School. Friends. Girls.

Our conversations consist of me asking questions and him giving one word answers about any of these subjects. Volleyball though, he'll expand.

Logan talks about his serve approach, spiking, and setting like they're the most important things in his life. When he talks about Coach Archer, however, my ears perk up and I find it hard to breathe.

The man has taken on God-like status with my son. He motivates Logan to do well on the court and in the classroom. My son wants to show he can outwork all the kids that have been playing in Coach Archer's club program since the sixth grade. Coach Archer supports and encourages Logan, and I like that.

What I don't like is that my heart does a tiny blip every time I hear the man's name. Nothing crazy. Just a small temporary spike in pace. It's ridiculous because not only is he a teacher at my son's school, and Logan's volleyball coach, he's much younger than me. Much, much younger.

I sit in the bleachers near two of the moms whose faces I recognize from years of attending back-to-school nights and school activities. We exchange smiles. I notice one of the women, Elaina, looks so put together I'd expect she prepared to strut down a runway.

Tight jeans hug her well rounded backside, and her shirt shows off enough cleavage for whispers to follow behind her. Her blonde hair is blown straight as a pin, and her make up looks as if it's been professionally airbrushed on.

The other mom, Lana is dressed a lot more casually, in a pair of yoga pants and a long shirt. Her hair is swept up in a ponytail, and her face is clear, devoid of any make-up.

"I swear, I'd give up manicures for a year to spend one night with him," Elaina leans over and whispers to Lana. "I mean, look at that ass. It's so round and tight. I bet he's big. Thick."

I want to hide my face. I can't believe she's saying these things out loud where people could hear her. It's nauseating.

Lana looks around to make sure no one overheard the inappropriate remark. I did. And I don't like it. I know who they're talking about, and they shouldn't be having those kinds of thoughts, let alone be verbalizing them.

Far too annoyed over this woman's obvious lust for Mr. Archer, which is none of my business, I turn from her and glance at the target of her desire. What annoys me more is that in his loose fitting jogging pants and the way his too tight t-shirt pulls across his broad, muscular chest, he's stirring up the same dark desires in me that he's encouraging in Elaina. At least she's brave enough to own them. Me, I bury them inside.

Before the boys take their places on the court, Mr. Archer gives each a few words and a pat on the shoulder. He takes a few seconds longer with Logan than he did with the other boys. I smile, appreciative of the extra attention he shows my son.

Logan responds to it, too. He doesn't talk much to me, but his body language changed. He stands taller and looks more confident. Thankfully, I haven't had any further calls from Mr. Butler. I can only think Mr. Archer is working some sort of magic on my son.

As if he knows what I'm thinking, or feels my eyes glued to him, Mr. Archer looks up and meets my stare. Caught, my face heats and fills with color. Shit, I'm probably redder than Elaina's lipstick.

I play it cool, look away and twirl a strand of blonde hair around my pointer finger. Not knowing what else to do, I look at the timer on the wall. Like I really care about the countdown until the start of the match.

I shouldn't feel so awkward, so self-conscious. After all, he's speaking to my son. I'm a mother. It's my responsibility to make sure there's nothing unsavory going on. Not that I think there is, but I have every right to pay attention to the interaction and make sure it's appropriate.

While true, I know this isn't why I'm unnerved. I can't fool myself into believing these excuses are why my stomach tumbles, and I find it hard to swallow. It's like high school all over again.

I try to brave another glance at Mr. Hotness. When my eyes land on him, they find him staring back. Deep blue eyes. Rough and tumultuous, like the ocean after a storm. Shit, I made a spectacle of myself and he noticed. I wonder who else noticed.

I look at the other parents around me. If anyone caught this interaction, no one lets on. Especially not Lana and Elaina. Thank goodness.

I can only imagine what he'll say to me after the meet. "I must say, Mrs. Collins, while I'm used to stares from the twelve year old girls I teach, I'm not used to seeing drool form around the mouth of my students 'mothers."

I want to disappear. This is bad. I hold my head, using my hands to shield my eyes like a set of blinders as I stare down at the ground. God, I don't want to see the look on his face and if I don't keep my eyes blocked, I'll look at him again.

As the event starts, I keep my eyes trained on the court in front of me where the opposing team serves the ball. I'm successful at keeping my eyes focused on the action, but I can't help from peeking at him at the end of every point. I tell myself it's just to see his reaction and make sure he's not coming down too hard on the boys. I know it's more than that.

If Mr. Archer would yell at the boys and act like a jerk when they make a mistake he wouldn't be so irresistible. No, instead he has to embody everything you'd want in a coach. He excites and encourages the boys, and judging by their performance, he's worked quite a bit on the fundamentals of the game.

Logan isn't a starter, and I'm not sure when he's going in because I don't know much about the game, but he looks perfectly happy standing on the side lines cheering his teammates on. Once he's on the court I'll have no problem keeping my eyes on him and off his sexy as hell coach.

Logan continues to move up in the line of boys on the side. He's next to get subbed in. I don't know how much time he'll get, but since he's brand new to the sport I'm glad he's being given a chance to learn and participate. Until a few weeks ago, I didn't know this was an option for middle school boys.

After the next point Logan jogs on the court as his friend Zach switches out. The boys high five as they pass each other. I rest my elbows on my knees and lean forward wanting to get closer. A tall boy on the team serves and it's an ace. We earn the point. The next serve is returned and Logan scrambles to get it. He does, but unfortunately the ball goes in the opposite direction of his teammates.

Logan stays in for another two points before rotating out. He doesn't step foot back on the court until the score is twenty to fifteen. Our team leads. A ball comes his way and this time he bumps to the front of the court the way he's supposed to. The ball gets set, then spiked over the net and we score.

I don't know who's smile is wider, mine or my sons.

We win the match three games to none. The cheering boys, bounce up and down on the court and gather around Coach Archer in celebration after the game. They still their bodies and listen intently to what the man has to say to them. Once he finishes, they grab their things and scramble in different directions.

Before Logan heads toward me, he shares a celebratory high five with Mr. Archer. I can't help the smile on my lips as Mr. Archer pats my son's back. Nor can I help my eyes from lingering on the man until Logan stands by my side.

I'm not prepared for the ear to ear smile on the coach's face when his eyes meet mine, or the heavy pounding in my chest at the wink of his eye. I think it's directed at me. At least I hope it is.

It can't be. I'm projecting my secret wish on him, that's all. But his eyes are focused on *me*.

I take a quick look around before meeting his stare again. Mr. Archer's smile widens as our eyes lock on each other once more. My stomach tumbles and swirls then tumbles again. Before I completely unravel like a teenager with her first crush, he turns and heads in the opposite direction.

The spell Mr. Archer has me under breaks. I take in a long breath. I need to pull myself together. For Logan. Breathing is the first step in slowing down my fluttering heart.

I feel the heavy weight of prodding eyes on me. I chance a quick glance over at Lana and Elaina who glare at me open mouthed. Shit. They must have caught that little exchange.

It's not like I did anything wrong. Mr. Archer is proud of Logan, the same way I am. That's all those looks meant. A mutual show of pride and respect.

Chapter 4

"Want to go to the diner to celebrate?" I ask Logan as he tosses his drawstring bag with his shoes and knee pads in the back.

"Okay," he sits down and buckles himself in.

"Steak?"

"You realize I didn't do much, right? I mean I lost more points for us then I helped get."

"Yes. But I'm proud. You just started playing."

"I only got one assist."

"That's why I want to get some protein in you to keep those muscles nice and strong." I give his bicep a squeeze.

"Stop!" He pulls his arm away from me and puts his ear buds in shutting down the conversation.

For a change, I'm okay with the silence between us. I don't have much to say, and the truth is, I want to run the heated looks and winks from Mr. Archer over in my mind. I shouldn't have gotten so happy with a little bit of attention.

Shouldn't have gotten all warm and gooey over it. I'm not fifteen.

The diner is packed. I notice only one empty table in the seating area and it happens to be next to us. After placing our orders Logan heads to the bathroom to wash his hands. I open the email on my phone. Two new authors contacted me regarding my proofreading rates.

I hate charging for something I love to do, but the money Keith left us won't last forever. It's not exactly dwindling, but the number in the bank decreases weekly and I have no way of replenishing it or holding it steady at a healthy level.

Eventually college won't be a someday away, it'll be tomorrow, and then today. I can't count on the current financial aid guidelines they have for children of single moms to not change for five years. That's too long of a time to think modifications won't be made, and too short of a time for me to pretend it's not racing up on us.

Logan ambles back aimlessly while the hostess seats someone at the table next to us. My son reminds me of a hearse driver, stoic and somber. He looks like he'd rather be anywhere else in the world than here with me.

"Anything exciting happen at school today?"

My son looks at me like I'm a creature from outer space.

"I'm in middle school, Mom," he answers like this is the most painful thing he's ever had to do. "Nothing exciting ever happens."

I sigh, defeated. I have nowhere to go. No direction to lead the conversation. I'm starting to wonder why I even bother trying anymore. Maybe I should just lay off and let him come around when he's ready. The thing is, if I take that approach, I'm not sure he'll ever be ready.

"Great job out there today."

Both our heads snap to the side to find Mr. Archer standing beside our booth. I'm thankful to see him, glad someone's here to break the awkward silence between my son and me. Even if it is only for a minute or two.

"Thanks. I know I didn't score, but at least I had an assist."

"You did your job. I bet your mom's proud."

"I am," I say with a smile so big my checks hurt.

Mr. Archer turns toward me and winks. Again. Warm blood flows around melting the ice in my veins. Now I know without a doubt, without question, the earlier one was directed at me.

The waitress sets down the plates with our food and scuttles off.

"I just wanted you to know I like the effort I'm seeing out there. It's the most important thing you can show a coach. As long as the effort is there, the skills will follow. Keep working hard." He looks over to the table next to us. The no longer empty table with his jacket slung over the back of a chair. "If you'll excuse me, I'll let you get back to your evening."

I glance at my son, then back at Mr. Archer. There seems to be a real connection between them. At least my son talks to his coach. More so than he does with me. They have actual conversations with give and take.

Without thinking my mouth opens and words slip out. "We'd love for you to join us, Mr. Archer."

"At school I'm Mr. Archer. Here, please, call me Mason."

A big smile spreads across Logan's face. "Sure thing, Mason."

"That was meant for your mom," his coach clarifies.

"Aww. That sucks," Logan complains.

"Please join us, Mason," I say, unsure of how I feel about this new development.

"Only if you're sure it's not an imposition." His blue eyes lock on mine again.

A wave of heat rushes through me sudden and strong. Sweat beads form on the back of my neck. This must be the part of menopause women complain about. I always thought the heat flashes were overplayed. Now I understand how uncomfortable it is.

I clear my throat because thinking about going through my changes while looking at Mason Archer is downright depressing.

"No." I smile. "No bother."

"You good with this, Logan?"

My son nods, and his coach excuses himself for a moment to grab his jacket and drink.

"You think the waitress will notice I moved over?" He asks Logan, sliding into the booth next to my son.

Logan shrugs and narrows his eyes. "I don't know. You think she's that smart? I mean she's just a waitress."

"Logan!"

MY SON DID NOT SAY THAT!

I can't look at Mason to see his reaction. I want to die, or at the very least slide down my seat and hide under the table. Seeing that I'm not made of a spineless gelatinous substance, I hang my head in shame. I can't believe Logan would look down on anyone willing to do honest work. Where the hell did this attitude come from?

Keith and I raised Logan to treat everyone with respect. From the janitor to the president, you don't differentiate in attitude based on title because you never know when the former will become the latter and vice versa.

What troubles me more is if that's what Logan thinks of the waitress, what does he think of me? I'm just a stay at home mom.

"Are you sure about that?" Mason asks. "I mean what if she's really a brain surgeon and she waits tables because she needs an escape from all the blood and gore she sees in the operating room?"

Logan shrugs.

"Or what if she knows all the secrets associated with deadly viruses and the CDC is after her to stop her from ever telling the public so she's hiding in plain sight?"

I'd never think of going down this road to get my point across. If Mr. Archer wasn't here, I'd probably lecture my son on how wrong it is to make a snap judgment about someone. I'd talk at him and he'd tune me out like he does with everything else.

"Or," Logan plays along. "What if she's on a mission to *infect* all the people with a deadly brain eating virus and she slips it into the food just so she can heal everyone later and be the hero?"

I'm captivated listening to my son and his coach go back and forth. It's the first time in years I've seen Logan so light hearted and silly. I enjoy the playful banter between them. Logan needs this. Not just the imaginative conversation, but the male bonding.

I'm glad Mr. Archer keeps the focus on Logan and doesn't ask me if I think the waitress will notice. I know she will. No heterosexual woman can be oblivious to a man like Mason Archer.

*

"I guess what I'm most curious about is why Logan wanted to start volleyball now, in eighth grade. No offense, but he never showed any interest in it before like he did with

~ 40 ~

baseball and football." I take a bite of my burger, trying to make conversation until my son gets back from the bathroom.

"That's my fault," Mason's eyes drop to the table for a moment. "I had Logan in my gym class when he first came to the school. We just started the program. I thought joining the team would be a good outlet for him with everything he had to deal with since there was no need for him to have played before. He wasn't ready then, but I knew eventually I'd convince him to give it a try."

"You were one of his sixth grade teachers?"

Mr. Archer's smile returns. Only it's not a happy smile. There's understanding and a tinge of something sad in his eyes.

He nods. "We met briefly when you came to school to share your concern for Logan over what happened to your husband."

"Oh, God." My hand shoots up to my mouth. I look away, embarrassed fighting the tears that spring to my eyes. "I'm so sorry. I don't remember you." I can't look at him. I feel like garbage admitting it. "I don't remember much from that time."

"It's fine." Mason reaches across the table and places his hand over mine. It's warm and rough and comforting as his thumb strokes the back of my hand. I look up and find his eyes locked on me. Another wave of heat rushes through my body. Maybe what I felt earlier wasn't a hot flash? Maybe it was a surge of hormones from the growing attraction I have for this man. An attraction I absolutely shouldn't feel.

"It was a tough time. I'm sure you felt like you were living in a fog for a while."

I'm awed. How does he know?

"I did. Sometimes I still do."

He gives me a sad smile as he pulls his hand away. I fight the urge to stop him and wrap my fingers around his. Confused and uncertain, I glance at my napkin and fiddle with the corners.

"If you find yourself wanting to talk to someone . . . Someone you can just vent to about how unfair the whole situation is . . . I'm a pretty good listener."

"Yeah, well." I keep my eyes down, too nervous and self-conscious to look at him. My heart's too full of emotion to meet his eyes. I shake my head. "I appreciate the offer Mr. Archer—"

"Mason."

"Mason." I'm confused when I hear the emotion I say his name with, "but I doubt you really want to hear me pour my heart out."

He leans forward, across the table. I lean in as well, like an invisible rope pulls me toward him. The distance between us shrinks by half and the air sparks with electricity as our eyes lock on one another.

"We all go through shit." He stares at me as if we are the only two people in the diner, until Logan snickers. My son returns from the bathroom just in time to hear his coach say an unsavory word.

Mason breaks the connection that had me sitting on the edge of my seat. He looks away, retreats with his arm slung over the back of the booth. The air around us thins. It's easier to breathe. "Some of us go through it sooner rather than later, that's all," he says as he moves into the corner making room for Logan to sit.

"You seem very wise for someone so young."

He laughs, and I like the sound. A lot. Deep. Sexy.

"Back to that, huh? Glad to see you're not one to hold my age against me."

Embarrassed, I drop my eyes to the empty dish in front of me. "Sorry. I didn't mean—"

"Don't be. I'm teasing. You might have noticed, I try not to take life too seriously."

I nod. Envying the easy, relaxed manner of the man across from me. I remember being young and carefree. What I wouldn't give to go back to that time.

"I might be a little younger than you—"

"A little?" I almost spit my soda out at him.

"*But* I know how important, how vital it is to have fun. And to have a support system. Sometimes it feels like people who haven't had a life changing experience put an artificial timer on your feelings. Like after a certain amount of time, you should be over it."

I'm floored by how spot on he is. He had to go through something of his own. I can't imagine what though. Or maybe he was there to help his mother through something, like Logan tries to help me. Shit. That must be it. It must have been his mother.

"How do you know?"

"I'm wise beyond my years," he teases.

"You're right, though. For some reason, my pain, my grief is like a burden to the people around me. Don't get me wrong, they were great in the beginning. I don't think I would have made it through without their support. But now that two years have passed, it's different. My best friend thinks I should get back out there and start dating. That I should just move on, like things didn't work out because Keith and I were fighting all the time and decided to break up."

"You're not ready." He states it as a fact. I'm not sure why, but it bothers me.

"I don't think it should be forced, you know? I mean if the right man were to come along, someone I wanted to go out with, that would be different. But just to find one for the purpose of not being alone. I can't do that."

He nods then turns to my son. "You know, Logan. I'm here for you, too."

I feel dismissed. I shouldn't, but I do. It smarts. I like the idea of having someone to talk to, to turn to. Maybe I said too much. Maybe I poured out more of my heart than he'd like to hear. If he can't handle that, there's no way in hell he wants to know how I really feel. How alone and heartbroken I am every second of the day.

"If you'll excuse me," Mr. Archer gets to his feet. Yep. I scared him off. Disappointment spreads across my chest. I want to take back what I said. I don't want him to leave the table. Moreover, I don't want to leave the diner and go back to an empty house. This was the nicest meal I've had since Keith died and I don't want it to be over. "I'll be right back."

Neither of us say anything as Logan's coach walks away. I make an effort to keep my eyes trained on my son and not follow the man who's so thoroughly captured my attention.

"Mr. Archer seems really nice. Is he this way with everyone?"

Logan shrugs. "He's okay."

"How was that steak?" We're back to forcing the conversation. This makes me realize just how much I enjoyed dinner. It's nice to have another person at the table to talk to. To engage my son, and laugh with. I don't know the last time it felt okay to laugh and smile. Or to just be me and not the phony I've become to placate the people that claim they care about me.

"Excuse me," I flag down the waitress as she passes by. "Can I have the check please?"

"Already taken care of," Mr. Archer says slipping back into the booth.

"You shouldn't have."

"I know." Mason smiles, and I feel myself turning into a warm sticky mess, again. What I really want to know is how do I keep him here? How do I keep the conversation going? "It's my way of thanking you for allowing me to crash dinner."

"That's not necessary. Really." I reach into my pocketbook. "Let me give you something towards it."

"Next Time. Tonight's my treat."

Next Time. Is he serious? I can't imagine the look on my face. I immediately look at my son to see his reaction. There isn't much of one. I guess that's good. He doesn't think much of the promise in Mr. Archer's comment. Me, I'm clutching it close to my chest with both hands. I only hope next Time comes fast.

Chapter 5

I sit by the fireplace finishing off the bottle of wine I opened when we got home. Logan's in his room playing guitar. His amp sounds like it's turned all the way up. I'm fine with it though because it's keeping us apart. I'm preoccupied and for a change I welcome the distance between us.

The letter with the findings of Mr. Butler's investigation came. Just as I expected, there's nothing there. I bet he was disappointed to find that my son is a good kid, and not the behavior problem he hoped for. I'm pissed that this is going down as a disagreement in which both boys were encouraged to seek guidance from Mr. Johnson after school for conflict resolution.

I flip through channels on the television. Nothing is on. Nothing that holds my interest. I sip wine from a glass and close my eyes, savoring the warmth as it slides down my throat. I've drank enough that my body's relaxed and my head light and tingly. I'm not drunk. I'm tipsy. Definitely tipsy.

Behind the lids of my eyes, I see an image of him burned into my memory. Mason. Sexy and strong. Smiling. The way his eyes danced and mesmerized me. The heat and tingling of his hand on mine. The pull he had on me at the diner.

I brush my hair back behind my ear. My hand slides down the side of my neck, and I imagine Mason touching me. His hand felt good over mine. Comforting. I wonder how his touch would feel in other places. Places I shouldn't be yearning to feel him.

I down the rest of the wine in my glass, say goodnight to my son and escape to the privacy of my bedroom. With my door shut, I lock it and turn down the lights. Even though I'm alone and have no reason to feel awkward or self-conscious, I do.

I picture Mason standing behind me and pull my shirt up over my head. I imagine the feel of his lips brushing down the side of my neck. His strong arms wrapping around me. Crushing me against his hard, sculpted body.

I open the hooks on my bra and slide my arms out letting it fall to the floor, pretending his rough, calloused hands move up and down my arms as my heavy breasts hang free. Bare. I'm not sure if it is the cool air or the heat of my thoughts that cause my nipples to perk up and harden. I welcome the prickling sensation.

I turn my focus back to Mason. If I remember correctly, his hands are a little rough, calloused. My breath catches as I think about the feel of those strong hands taking hold of my breasts squeezing greedy handfuls and teasing them with his fingers and mouth.

I close my eyes, longing for him. For the heat of his body against mine as I unbutton my pants and slide them down my legs. I run my pointer finger across my bottom lip, wondering how far I'm willing to take this.

A familiar ache I haven't felt in ages presents itself between my legs. An ache bred of need and desire. An ache I've been numb to for the past two years. It grows inside me with each breath.

I drag my finger down my neck, down my sternum. Straight down to the waist band of my panties. My heart races. My lower abdomen tightens. It's hard to breathe. I trace the band of my lace panties, thinking about Mason touching me, goose bumps cover my skin.

My entire body is taut with need, and desire. For the first time since I met my husband, I yearn for the physical comfort and release of another man. I think about letting go of my inhibitions and exploring my body. My face burns hot with the knowledge of what I'm imagining.

Tossing my panties on the side of the bed, I lie on my back and search for the courage to open my petals and touch myself while one thought consumes me, Mason.

I bite my lip, imagining the feel of his strong muscular chest. Thinking about his tight round ass. I pretend he's naked, in bed with me. One hand clenches the sheets beneath me as the other finds my breast and pinches my nipple.

A slight moan leaves my mouth and brings me back to the moment. I freeze. What am I doing fantasizing about another man? A younger man? Ashamed, I pull the covers up to my chest to cover myself. It doesn't matter that I'm alone in bed, I still feel the need to hide my body.

My heart swells with guilt. It's wrong to think of another man in this way. To have a primal desire for anyone but Keith. I miss him. *God, do I miss him.*

He's was my best friend. My lover. My other half. And I'll never see him again. Never hear the sound of his voice, or my name slipping off his lips. He'll never sneak up from behind and wrap me up in his arms while kissing the back of my neck. He'll never whisper my name as he nibbles on my ear. He'll never touch me. Never again.

A fresh wave of emotion gut punches me. It hurts too much. I don't want to breathe. I don't feel whole anymore. I'm hurt and angry. So damn angry. It's not fair. We were supposed to grow old together. Holding hands and making memories.

We shared everything. We were partners in every way, and he was taken from me. Stolen. Our future, snatched from our hands because some drunk thought he could drive.

What I wouldn't give for five minutes alone with that monster. I'd rip his eyes out and feed them to him.

I can't believe what I almost did. I know that it's no big deal. It's nothing I haven't done before. It's natural. My heart won't accept that. My wedding band hugs my finger and I'm fantasizing about another man. I'm the worst wife ever. Wanting Mason to touch me in intimate ways, longing to feel him inside me feels like I'm cheating not only on Keith's memory, but on him as well.

Tears pool and spill out of my eyes. I can't stop them. I don't want to. The pain of losing my husband hangs over me at all times, but right now, I'm drowning in it. Suffocating. I reach for the framed picture I keep on my night table.

Oh God. He watched me the whole time. Watched me try to touch myself while lusting over Mason Archer.

"I'm sorry," I whisper through the emotion in my throat. "I'm so sorry, baby."

He doesn't answer. He never does. I should be used to it. Only now I'm taking that silence as disappointment. Disapproval.

I feel dirty. Disgusting. I need to shower and wash away the guilt. It's all I can do to get myself up and into my bathroom. I let the hot water fall and pelt my skin. I make it hotter, so hot it hurts. Scalds. Until I can't take anymore. I dry myself off, slip my nightgown on and climb back to bed.

Not feeling any better, I continue my conversation with Keith and beg for his forgiveness. I ugly cry, muting my sobs as much as I can so that Logan doesn't hear.

I cry feeling alone. Empty. I have no one in my life to hold me and soothe the heartache. No one to tell me sweet lies that it will get easier and I'll be okay. I cry until my swollen eyes close and sleep carries me to another realm.

Chapter 6

I frown checking the time. I'm running late to pick Logan up from practice. I needed a few things at the grocery store. My quick trip took longer than I expected. If I knew I'd get stuck behind a woman that would challenge the price of every item she self-scanned, I would've skipped the ice cream.

The desert already feels soft and drippy. I try to salvage the cookies and cream so that it doesn't turn into a sweet milky mess and drop the groceries off at home instead of driving straight to school. I leave my car running in the garage while I plop the bags on the counter and stuff my decadent surprise in the freezer.

Racing back to the car, I gasp and almost fall over my feet as they come to a dead stop while the momentum from the top part of my body moves forward. It's gone! My running car, and everything inside it, including my pocketbook and cell phone.

Gone. Without a trace. Like they disappeared into thin air. Only they couldn't have. Which means while I was fifty feet away in the kitchen, with nothing but an unlocked door between us, someone came into my garage, sat their ass in the driver's seat and drove off with my car.

I run out of the garage and down to the lip of the driveway turning my head from side to side, as if this will somehow make it reappear. Not only doesn't my car magically drop on the ground in front of me, but I don't even catch a glimpse of it speeding off.

I hug my arms around my pounding chest feeling vulnerable. Violated. What's worse is I have no way to get to Logan. No way to call any friends and ask for a favor because I don't remember anyone's phone number. They're all programmed into my cell phone.

"Shit!" I run my hands through my hair, close my eyes and remind myself to take a breath.

I have a landline. I hardly use it, but it's a phone. The only numbers programmed in it are family. Mine and Keith's. And Logan's cell phone!

While I still have no way to get him home; Keith's family lives a couple of hours away in neighboring Pennsylvania, and my parents are in south Jersey so they wouldn't make it here in less than an hour. At least I could let Logan know what's going on.

The last thing I want is to hold Mr. Archer up any longer. Then I'll feel obligated to personally apologize. We haven't spoken since sharing dinner together at the diner and I'd like to keep it that way. I can't handle the feelings he stirs up inside me.

I'll call Logan and have him ask a friend to pick him up and give him a ride home. That should work. And the best part is I can continue my streak of avoiding Mr. Archer. Three weeks and counting, go me!

If only I can find a way to stop thinking about the man. During the games I force myself to keep my wandering eyes focused on the court and not on the sidelines, and then I leave the building the second the last point is scored. The few times that we've made eye contact, I break it immediately. Things are better this way. No good can come of me lusting over Mason Archer.

While I see my son improving, he still struggles and spends more of his time on the sidelines than on the court. I try to use that as a reason to dislike the man consuming too much time in my head.

"Mom, why are you home?" Logan asks answering his phone. "I've been texting you. You're late. Everyone's gone."

I clear my throat and work hard to keep my voice calm and steady. "Logan, honey, the car was stolen."

"Stolen?"

"Yep. And my pocketbook and phone are in the car."

"Oh shit! Was it a carjacking? Are you okay?" Fear colors his voice.

"No, sweetie. Nothing like that. But I don't have any way to get to you. Can you call Zach or one of your other friends and see if their mom can give you a ride home? I don't have anyone's number."

"Yeah. Sure. I'll see you in a little bit."

I hang up and take a deep breath before calling the police. That went better than I thought.

With nothing left to do but wait, I climb the three steps that lead to my front door and sit on the top one. I wait for my son. For the police. For whoever stole my car to return it and say it was a terrible mistake.

A police car pulls up without the pomp and circumstance of lights and sirens. I take a deep breath and ready myself for what comes next. I get to my feet as two uniformed officers climb out of one car and a second police car pulls up. Lucky me, now I get to confess to multiple officers I'm stupid enough to leave the car running while unattended.

Two officers examine the garage and the perimeter of the house while the other two officers get the pertinent information from me. We start with the easy questions first, then move on to what happened.

"Mom!"

I turn at the sound of my son's voice. He rushes toward me and almost knocks me down wrapping his arms around me. I kiss his head and stroke his hair.

"Hey, buddy. I'm okay."

"Are you sure?"

He looks up at me, eyes wide and frightened. For a moment, I lose time. He's not the brooding thirteen year old that shuts me out at every turn. He's my baby boy. I want to hold on to this moment.

"I'm better now that you're here," I smile and squeeze him for emphasis. How did you get here? Who gave you a ride?"

As I ask the question, I look up and see Mason Archer walking towards us. My heart thrums in time with his steps. I can't believe he's here. This must have put a wrench in his plans for the evening. I feel awful.

"Mr. Archer," I say as the man approaches. "I'm sorry. I didn't mean to hold you up."

"How are you?" He looks annoyed, maybe even angry, as his dark, turbulent eyes look me over.

"I'm fine," I rub my forehead. "I ran in the house for a minute and left the car running. Stupid, I know. But I do it all the time. So do my neighbors. Nothing like this has ever happened."

"Finish with cops. Logan and I will wait over there." He nudges his head toward the steps leading to my front door. I watch for a breath happy he's here, while he leads my son away.

I continue answering questions, while two officers walk through the house to make sure it's empty then check with the neighbors to see if anyone saw or heard anything unusual, and if they might have any useful video from their doorbells since I don't.

Once they're done gathering information, the lead officer hands me a card with his name, number and contact information on it. He ticks off a list of action items for me to do; inform the insurance company, order a replacement driver's license online, cancel all credit and debit cards, disable the garage door, and change the locks.

Overwhelmed, I watch the group of officers reconvene at their cars parked in front of my house.

Startled, I let out a high pitched gasp at the soft touch on the small of my back. I look next to me and take a deep breath one part relieved to find worried blue eyes staring back at me, and one part undone because with my nerves already compromised I can't hide or control the shaking of my body now that he's near.

"Mason, thank God." My heart gallops in my chest beneath my hand.

"How are you holding up?" He whispers, causing shivers to run through me.

"I'm okay. I mean I wasn't in the car or anything."

Mason takes a step closer to me, forcing me to look in his eyes "That doesn't mean you're okay."

"Oh." He's asking about my mental state. I peek over to where I last saw my son, wondering how he feels about his hot coach standing so close and talking so intimately with me.

"Logan wanted to go check on his room, make sure nothing's missing. I didn't think you'd mind since the police already checked out the house."

"No. Of course not." Shaking, I hug my arms around myself.

"You're really shaken up." He says as if I'm an open book and he's on chapter four.

Unable to find the strength to lie, I nod.

"I'm here."

Mason reaches for one of my trembling hands. My nerves have the best of me. Only now, I'm not sure what's affecting me more, his touch, or the fact that almost everything of importance to me has been stolen. I feel lost, like earth opened and sucked me into the depths of a deep dark hole.

"I . . . I don't even know . . . where or how . . ."

"You have no car." I look up, noticing for the first time how close Mason stands to me. Close enough that I have to tilt my head back to meet his eyes. Close enough that I feel his body heat gathering around me and warming me like a blanket. "And a lot to do. I'll help."

Tempted to decline his offer, I realize I have no way to do everything on my own. I can't even rent a car until my credit cards are replaced because you need to have one on record. I know my parents will help but when I tell them they're going to freak out from worry. I'm already wrecked, I don't have it in me to reassure them.

"You're right. There is a lot to do."

He shoves his hands deep in his pockets and stands to his full height, chest out. "Then let's get to it."

The way he says it, so strong and matter of fact, he leaves no room for discussion. I don't bother to protest. For a change I don't want to play the part of the strong independent woman. I'm not up to it right now. I've played that part for the last two years. I'd like a reprieve, and I like who's giving it to me even more.

Chapter 7

Before we make it inside the house I stop short as the cool breeze carries a whiff of cologne straight to my nose. It's subtle, a little outdoors, mixed with a tinge of spice, but it's undeniably Mason. I feel the need to say something and extend this moment.

"Won't you get in trouble for bringing Logan home?"

"Only if someone saw." Mason takes his jacket off and wraps it around my shoulders. I pull it tighter around me, getting high on his scent. My chest tightens. I shouldn't like being this close to him. I shouldn't enjoy how comfortable I feel around this man, how much I enjoy the little touches, or the intoxicating feeling I get when he looks at me and smiles. "Doesn't matter though. It was my choice to throw him in the car. I'll deal with the consequences."

Who is this man?

"Mr. Archer . . ." His eyebrow shoots up as he stabs me with a pointed look. "Mason, I don't want to cause any trouble for you."

"How else was he going to get here? He turned white when he spoke to you. It was the right thing to do." His thumb presses on his bottom lip, reminding me of how much I'd like to get acquainted with those lips. "I'd do it again in a heartbeat."

Heartbeat. Does he have any idea he has mine racing and jumping hurdles?

I fight the sudden urge to throw myself against his chest, lay my head on his shoulder and breathe him in. I shouldn't think like this, want any of this because he's my son's coach. That's not even the worst part. Mason Archer is at least a decade younger than me, if not two, and the more time I spend around him, the more I allow myself to fantasize about something happening between us.

I don't know how or where it started. It's wrong on so many levels. I never even noticed younger men. Until a few weeks ago when Mr. Archer stopped to speak to me on the school steps.

He inches closer and holds the lapel of the jacket. My brain short circuits. I'm so fried between the car being stolen and his proximity, I can only stare in silence pretending I understand what he's saying as his full pouty lips move.

His teeth graze his bottom lip a moment before he continues. "Don't worry, beautiful. I've got this."

He called me beautiful! Birds and butterflies come to life in my belly. They race and soar. I don't protest any further.

It feels good to have someone help pick up the broken pieces around me for a change.

"Come on," Mason places his big, strong hand on my lower back. "Lead the way." He gestures with his other hand.

As we continue the few feet to the front door I peek at Mason through the corner of my eye. He's calm, cool and in control. Not to mention sexy as hell. His confidence has me mesmerized. Under a spell. Once again I feel like a teenager with her first crush.

As I turn the door knob his hand slips from my back and moves around my waist. He pulls me against him. My hand drops. I'm not sure what to do with it.

Mr. Archer stands still a moment, keeping me frozen in place. His breath tickles my ear as he moves in closer. My heart pounds like a drum in my chest. His mouth is alongside my ear as he reaches for the knob to open the door for me.

"Don't push me away," he whispers sending shivers down my spine once again. "Let me help you."

It's hard to speak or even swallow when he keeps taking my breath away like this.

*

The second we step inside my house it hits me. This relationship, or whatever it is just reached a new level. Mason Archer's standing in my living room!

He fills every ounce of empty space. I'm nervous and excited and completely unsure of myself. It's like having a boy in my bedroom for the first time all over again. I don't know what to do or how to act.

"Well?" He asks, but I have no clue what he's asking.

I clear my throat before I speak. I don't want him to suspect I'm interested, even though right now interested doesn't even scratch the surface of what I am. After the stress of having my car stolen and the surprise of Mason showing up to help out, I'd love for him to pin me against a wall and kiss me senseless. Maybe do a lot more than kiss me.

Of course that won't happen. It *can't* happen with my son in the next room. Which makes me want it even more. Mason is forbidden fruit.

"Well what?" I answer too nervous to look at him. Too embarrassed by my unsavory thoughts.

"Where should we start?"

The wall, the couch, the floor come to mind. But that's not what he means.

Where the hell are these thoughts coming from? I've never been this type of girl. Never lusted after anyone like this. Never fantasized about having sex with anyone while I pleasured myself. At least not anyone that isn't my husband.

Wasn't my husband.

Guilt hugs my heart like a boa constrictor hugs a mouse. How can I yearn for something to happen *here?* In the house I shared with Keith?

Keith.

Thoughts of my husband sober my longings. We spent time as a family in this room, talking and watching television. On rare occasions when we were lucky enough to find ourselves alone in the house, we'd end up naked taking advantage of the solitude. But being with Keith in that way isn't an option. It won't be ever again.

I shouldn't feel so conflicted about moving on. According to my friends and family it's what I'm supposed to do. Get back on that horse. As if.

"I don't know." I run my hands through my hair.

Maybe if Mason was an average guy and not the hottest man in a small town I'd feel better about the situation and the sexual longings I have for him.

But he's not an average guy. That is part of the attraction. He's young and hot. And insanely sexy. Sex drips off him, like water off your hair when caught in an unexpected downpour.

"Why don't you start with the insurance company and bank, and I'll call a locksmith."

He flashes me a smile. The one that invites me to explore his mouth. I nod, but he doesn't move. He rubs his thumb on his bottom lip that I want to kiss and taste more than anything at the moment.

"Sounds good." I turn and head into the other room to look for my insurance policy.

Putting in my claim will help me ignore the tingling that crawled up my legs and settled into my lower half and the guilt I have for wanting to use this man to fulfill my sexual desires. I shouldn't be so focused on these things when he just did a kind deed for me.

I'm objectifying him like a pervy old man does when he sees a pretty young woman in a bikini. Part of me really doesn't care because after not having these thoughts and feelings for so long, it feels good. I feel alive and I want to keep having them. God, I'm pathetic. I'm worse than a horny old man.

I'm a horny old woman!

While on hold my mind races back to Mason. I want to show him my appreciation for his kindness, do something nice for him. Call me crazy but I don't think a lap dance will qualify. Besides, I'd probably bore him. No, it has to be something that says thank you, but isn't over the top. I'm not sure what though. Dinner? Bake him some cookies? Sure, just like a gray haired grandma. Maybe I could knit him a hat and socks while I'm at it.

I focus on the business at hand when a live person takes me off of hold. I give her my personal information and answer questions, aware that Logan and Mason are talking in the other room. I hear a door close and wonder if my son is upset that Mr. Archer is still here.

With my back to the doorway, I feel Mason behind me. He oozes warmth and strength and this man must be putting out supernatural pheromones because I've never been this sexually aware of another person.

My mind buzzes and I can't think straight. Maybe I could if these darn butterflies would go hibernate and stop fluttering like mad in my stomach when he's near. Although if they stop, the birds might fly south for the winter, and with anymore feeling down there I won't be responsible for my actions.

He stays silent until I hang up. He looks at his phone. And my stomach drops realizing, he's probably checking for a message from his wife or girlfriend. That thought sets me straight.

"Thank you." I break the awkward silence between us. "For everything."

"No worries. I'm glad to help." He smiles, but it doesn't reach his eyes.

Something's off and I'm not sure what it is or where it came from. It wasn't here a few minutes earlier. Either something transpired with Logan, I'm right about the wife or girlfriend, or he wants to keep me at an arm's length and let me know he isn't interested in me in the lustful-I'm-barely-keeping-my-hands-off-you way I'm interested in him.

Oh, no! What if he can read my thoughts? What if he *knows* I'm thinking about him in *that* way? That I enjoy watching the way his muscles ripple and tease through his clothes when he moves. Or that since Logan left us alone I can't stop wondering how Mason looks with his clothes off. How his naked body would feel against mine. Rubbing. Touching. Caressing.

"You don't have to stay." I give him an out. He's already gone above and beyond what anyone else would've done for me. I don't want him to feel obligated to babysit me, too. "I can call a friend or my parents."

His blue eyes narrow and singe a hole in my heart. A tiny hole with his name written all over it. A hole a piece of him crawls in and fills.

"Trying to get rid of me?"

"No." I shake my head. "Not at all. I just—"

"Shh." He holds his pointer finger up and steps forward. Close. Inches away, I feel his energy mesh with mine like entwined fingers. I expect him to touch my lips and wait for it.

I tremble. My heart races. I feel Mason's warmth and strength as he reaches his hands under my hair and holds the back of my neck. My head tilts up slightly. I wonder, if he'll kiss me. *Please kiss me*. My lips part.

His touch feels so good. Electric. Energized. *Right.*

My breaths deepen in anticipation of what's coming next. I imagine him, will him, to lean in and meet my lips with his, but he's given no indication that he wants to kiss me. Except for the fact that he's so close, and hasn't taken his eyes off me.

"You hanging in there?" His eyes pierce mine. They're intense and beautiful, and I just want to stand here and stare into them. Maybe forever.

"Of course. Besides, it's not like I really have a choice."

He lets go of my head, and takes my hands into each of his. He lifts and studies them in the same way.

"You're not shaking anymore."

Maybe on the outside. On the inside every nerve vibrates from his touch.

"The shock wore off."

"Good." He says, his voice warm and velvety.

And then nothing.

For a few long beats, he doesn't move. Doesn't say anything. He just stares into my eyes. The weight of the moment builds. It's heavy. Palpable. I can't breathe.

"You know, you still haven't told me your name."

"I haven't?"

He shakes his head. "I could call you Mrs. Collins if that's the way you want to play it." He smirks and raises his eyebrows playfully. "Or I could look at Logan's participation form, but I want you to tell me. I want to hear it from your luscious lips."

Hearing him say those words causes dampness to rush to the area between my legs. Like dry kindling, the air around us crackles and sizzles with every look. Every touch.

I clear my throat, but my voice is still heavy. "Amber."

"A beautiful name for a beautiful woman." He holds my head again, and rubs his thumbs back and forth across my cheeks." The touch is gentle. Intimate. A completely inappropriate way for my son's coach to touch me.

He breathes hard. His eyes smolder. I stare at his full, pouty lips. The idea of him kissing me seems like it might actually happen. While I want him to because I long to be touched and desired, especially by him, I'm torn.

I don't think I'll be good at it. I haven't kissed anyone but Keith in almost two decades. And no one in two years. That makes me feel old.

Very old.

Being attracted to this young man and wanting him to want me in return, feels wrong. Shame and guilt swell inside me.

I dart my eyes away from his breaking the connection. This way I can hide any doubts or negativity he might find there. Keeping my eyes off him also helps me stay strong so I don't throw myself against him, wind my fingers through his hair and pull his head down to meet my lips. I can't do that, because I enjoy this connection with him too much to risk doing anything that might sever it.

His face inches in a bit closer. I meet him half way. That I can do, but he has to initiate it. I inhale and stay focused on his eyes, and not the warmth of his breath brushing against my lips.

Centimeters separate us. I stand perfectly still. I don't move. I don't close the distance any further because I'm afraid. I want to kiss him more than anything at this moment, but the thought terrifies me.

Turns out, I don't have to worry about it. Mason lets go of me, drops his eyes, and reaches for his phone. The moment is gone, and I'm crushed. Overwrought with disappointment. Because I doubt either of us will allow things to get so heated again. It would be Irresponsible. Dangerous.

"C'mon," he motions his head toward the door. "Your chariot has arrived."

"My chariot?"

He smirks and steps away.

I take a few deep breaths as I follow him. Mason stops suddenly and turns back to face me. I don't realize he's no longer moving, and bump into a wall of warmth and thick, solid muscle. His hands grasp and hold my upper arms as he steadies me and searches my eyes once more.

"I want to kiss you, Amber. You need to know that. It's taking every ounce of self-control not to bend down and taste your sweet lips right now."

"Why? I mean why not? I mean . . ."

He holds my chin between his thumb and forefinger, tilting my head up. "Because," he cuts me off. "I'm afraid you're not ready, and if I move too fast, you'll shut down and push me away."

"Why does it matter?"

"Because it does. Now don't look so disappointed. Just know that when the time is right, I'm going to kiss you long and hard while I hold you pressed up against me. And when I do, I'll work my hardest to make sure you're not thinking about anything but that kiss. Our first kiss. And I have no intention of it being our last kiss."

I nod.

"And one more thing, Amber. It's going to be the best kiss of your life."

Chapter 8

"Thank you, but I can't drive this." I look at the shiny black Mustang parked in my driveway. I don't know what strings Mason pulled, but I'm too pre-occupied and unnerved by his promise a moment ago to understand what accepting this means.

"Yes, you can. You need a car, I got a car for you. Problem solved."

After circling the car three times, Logan joins us in time to hear me decline the very generous car Mason's friend dropped off. My son's eyes light with excitement.

"C'mon, Mom, all my friends at school will be jealous," Logan insists.

"It's not practical. And you won't be the one driving it."

"Who cares? It's lit. Please, Mom?"

"Don't say no before taking it for a ride." Mason challenges.

"I can't drive without a license."

"Which you'll go online and replace in a few minutes."

Before I can effectively argue back, the locksmith pulls up.

"We're not done discussing this," Mason says as I walk away to show the locksmith the three locks that need to be changed. "C'mon, Logan. Let me show you how to change a garage door opener." *Where the hell did he get a garage door opener?*

Over the last year I considered changing the locks so I'd have keyless entry into the house from wherever I am, but I didn't plan to do in an emergency situation with an emergency fee attached to it. This is one mistake I'm going to feel in my pocket big time.

I leave the locksmith to take on another task. Before hopping online to report my license stolen and print out a copy, I call the bank and cancel my debit card. I learn that they're trying to contact me via my cell phone regarding suspicious activity. Turns out I have a seven hundred dollar charge to a bathhouse. Who goes to a bathhouse these days?

Once I claim it's a fraudulent charge, they promise to shut the card down and send me a new one in three days. Great. I search the kitchen for the most recent credit card statements I saved. Luckily there are only two and it only takes half an hour to close the accounts and have replacement cards sent.

The locksmith calls me over to enter the code. I know better than to use a birthday or anniversary. Maybe that's for the best, the last thing I need to do is force Keith to the front of my mind every time I open the door. That won't help my quest to move forward.

While setting the code on the garage door, I take a quick peek at Mason standing on a ladder. Logan's close by, ready to hand him a tool. Maybe my friends and family are right and it is time to get out there and start dating. Logan sure seems to enjoy spending quality time with another man.

*

"Are you ready?" Mason asks with a smirk.

"Please, Mom. Please!" I don't remember the last time I saw my son so excited. I can't say no.

"Get out of your comfort zone. What's the harm in trying something new?"

The question feels loaded. Like he's talking about more than the car. The rise of his eyebrow confirms it. In the next heartbeat Mason tosses the keys at me. Instinctively I reach up and catch them mid-air.

"Fine. We can take it for a ride, and then you can call your friend and tell him to take it back. I'm sure a car like this is way out of my budget. I can only pay what the insurance company is going to give me."

Mason smirks. He's cocky and self-assured and I want to smack that look off his face. With my lips.

"I don't think it's as far out of reach as you think," he says as we head out. "We'll see what we can work out if you like it."

~ 75 ~

Mason presses a button on the key fob. He opens the driver's side door for me and leans on the frame. Draped on the door like that he reminds me of a television game show model showing off prizes. He's definitely in the wrong profession. He should be selling cars at a for-women-only lot. He'd be raking in the money because he looks even sexier like this than usual, and I didn't think that was possible.

I hate that all Mason needs to do is lean on something and stare at me to make me feel warm and gooey inside. He fixes his eyes on mine, and I wonder if he does that because he knows it makes me tingle all over.

I sit behind the wheel, and adjust the seat and mirrors. I'm nervous to drive. I shouldn't be, but I can't afford the repairs if anything happens to this car. I take a deep breath then ease off the brake, backing out of my driveway.

"Take it on the highway," Mason instructs after I drive a few blocks.

"I don't know." I want to, but I have no intention of keeping the car.

"C'mon, Mom, do it! Do it!"

"Fine."

Sitting in the driver's seat, I enjoy the power of the engine when I accelerate. It doesn't take much for the engine to pick up speed with a muted roar. The wheel is super responsive when I make an adjustment. I'm surprised when I look at the speedometer. We're doing eighty down the highway. I have no idea I'm driving this fast. Mason is right. This car is fun to drive. A lot of fun.

I feel something I haven't in a long time. Young and free. The only problem I'll have driving this car is that I might not want to give it back.

"So what do you think?"

"I like it, but like I said, I'm not sure I can afford . . ."

"It won't cost you anything."

"You can't ask that of your friend. Business is business."

"It's my car. I'm selling it. I thought I'd get some good exposure at his shop where people might be in the market to buy when they find out how much fixing their car will be. I can wait a few more weeks until your insurance company sends you the money for a new car."

"I can't."

"Can't or don't want to?"

"Both." Something akin to guilt fills my chest and wrings my heart. Accepting this would be taking advantage of him.

"Why not?"

"It's yours."

"You considered it when you didn't know it was mine."

"You're selling it. You need the money. What if something happens to it? I'd feel terrible, and I wouldn't be able to replace it."

"I don't need the money. Don't get me wrong, it's nice to have extra cash, but I'm fine financially. The car was a gift, so it's been paid off for years. Right now it's just collecting dust because no one is using it. And if anything happens, that's what insurance is for."

I open my mouth, but before I can utter a word, he interrupts me. "I'm loaning it to you, that's all. No strings attached."

I don't speak for a few seconds. I let his words sink in. He makes it sound simple. Maybe it is that simple and I'm just making too much of it. Part of me is disappointed with his no strings comment. I sort of wish he'd want something from me sexually in exchange for use of the car.

I want to hit my head. Something is wrong with me. I hate that he's awakened the sexual part of my brain. No doubt it expects my body to follow suit.

"Okay," I agree.

"Great. Now, let's go for pizza. None of us have eaten, and I'm sure Logan's hungry. He worked up an appetite at practice today."

More time with Mason Archer. That's music to my ears. I work to keep my face blank so he won't know my insides are wiggling and jiggling like gelatin on a trampoline.

*

In an attempt not to run into any of his students, Mason suggests going for pizza a few towns over. It's only a fifteen minute drive, but decreases the likely hood of running into anyone either of us know.

Logan's very talkative over dinner. He dominates the conversation with useless facts about Italy, pizza and how it's made. Turns out his "friend" Delaney brought homemade pizza into school for him to try. She's taking an Italian cooking class and brings him samples of the things she cooks. Right now cooking is her go to activity. I can think of a lot worse.

I know she means a lot to my son from his enthusiasm. He's never been one to get excited over eating. Sure he likes when I bake treats for him, but he's never, not one time, gone on about anything I made the way he's going on about Delaney's pizza.

"The crust was amazing. It wasn't just a regular crust. I mean it was but it sort of tasted like a garlic knot. I've never had crust like that. It was almost as good as her bread. The bread was different though. It was sweet and almost tasted like the bread grandma makes for Easter. And next week she starts working on desserts. She's going to make cheesecake and cannolis."

Logan goes on and on. I listen in fascination, curious about this girl, and why he hasn't mentioned one thing about her before now. I haven't seen his eyes shine like this since . . . his father was alive.

"Delaney is a really nice girl," Mason says, as if he knows where my mind is going. "When you meet her, I think you'll like her."

It bothers me that Mason knows more about the girl Logan's crushing on than I do. And clearly Logan doesn't have a problem talking to his coach about her. When I bring Delaney up, I get shot down.

"Why would Mom meet her?"

"Because she's your friend. And I like getting to know your friends," I answer.

"Yeah, but not girls, Mom. C'mon, you don't need to know every girl I talk to."

"From the way it sounds, she's not just a girl you talk to. She sounds like a lot more than that."

"Jeez, I didn't know being friends with a girl is such an issue for you."

I have no idea where this attitude is coming from, but I don't like it. I'm about to unleash everything I've kept bottled up since I found out my car had been stolen on my ungrateful son, when Mason beats me to it.

"Logan, you need to watch your tone."

"Whatever." My son gets up and stalks off to the bathroom.

I consider following after him, but I know that won't do an ounce of good. I'll end up making a scene and the last thing I want to do right now is draw attention to the fact that we're here with Mr. Archer. If there is anyone from the neighborhood that recognizes us, rumors will run like wildfire in school.

"Will you be okay for a minute?" Mason asks, his eyes glued to Logan.

"Yeah, fine," I lie.

Mason follows after my son. I guess that's better than me going bat-shit-crazy in front of everyone. Alone at the booth, I use the opportunity to pay the bill with my secret stash cash I grabbed at home before we left. It's a small token for all the help Mason's given me tonight.

The guys come back laughing, and like a disappearing act in a magic show, the attitude that crawled up my son's behind is gone without a trace. I guess whatever happens in the bathroom stays in the bathroom.

"You want to tell your mom, or should I?"

Logan shrugs, then jumps in and beats Mason to the punch.

"Mr. Archer's going to work with me for extra practice on Saturdays."

"I know the season is almost over," Mason works his blue eyes on me, and has my full attention. "I don't have as much time to work with Logan individually during practice as I'd like, but if you don't mind, I'm happy to give him a little one on one time on Saturdays."

"And you want to do this?" I ask my son.

"Are you for real?" Logan's eyes grow to twice their normal size. "I would love it. And this way I have a real shot at making the high school team next year." His excitement is infectious. I feel it bubbling up around me. Or maybe that's my own excitement because I know I'm going to be seeing a lot more of Mason Archer.

Chapter 9

I pull into my driveway. No one moves to get out of the car. Seconds pass in silence. I think they turn to minutes. It feels like it, but I'm certain that's just because I'm nervous and feeling unsure of myself. I expect Logan to rush to get out, but he doesn't.

"Hey, Mr. Archer, were you ever in a band?" If I didn't know better, I'd think my son is trying to keep his coach here. Looks like none of us are ready for the night to end.

"Nah, I'm not what you'd call musically inclined. Sports were my thing."

"Oh." Logan goes on for about five minutes, telling Mason the plans he has to put a band together, and how he wants to market it.

When my son is finished, I jump in. "Would you like to come in for coffee?" I ask through a yawn.

"I'd love to, but I think I should let you get some rest. It's been a long day."

I want to protest, tell him I have too much adrenaline pumping through me, mixed with lustful thoughts of him. There's no way I'm going to rest. Instead, I agree.

Mason opens the glove box and checks to make sure the insurance and registration are where they are supposed to be.

"Take my cell. This way if you have any questions about the car," his eyes turn toward the back seat, "you can call me."

"G'night, Mr. Archer," Logan says getting out of the car and heading for the house.

"Night, Logan." Mason answers.

We are alone.

Just the two of us. Sitting in the car which suddenly feels very small and cramped, yet we are far apart.

Mason reaches for the phone in my hands, and taps away at the keyboard. Before handing it back, his phone chimes.

"This way I have your number," he grins as he opens the car door and looks back at me, "And Amber, I want you thinking about what that kiss would've been like earlier when you go to bed tonight." Without another word, he gets to his feet and heads to his car.

I want to respond, but I can't, he doesn't give me the opportunity. Besides what is there to say? He caught me off guard.

I'm just grateful the car door was open or else the windows might've fogged up from the sudden burst of heat spreading through my body. He did that on purpose. He had to.

I enter the house through the front door, and head into the kitchen. Logan stands there staring, waiting for me.

"What's up, Buddy?"

"I don't know, Mom. You tell me." he sounds annoyed. I feel a nervous twisting in my stomach. I think I know what he's talking about, but I play dumb. Just in case I'm wrong.

"I don't know what you're getting at."

"What's the deal with Mr. Archer?"

"He's your coach, and he's looking to help you out."

"What's the deal with *you* and him?"

I swallow hard.

"There's no deal, Logan. He's a nice man and we are sort of becoming friends." It's not a lie I whisper to my conscious because it's wreaking havoc in my mind.

"Good. As long as you're just friends."

"Did you think something else is going on?" I'm not sure what I'm hoping for him to say.

"No. At least I hoped not."

"You don't like him?"

"No. I like him. But everyone would laugh. You'd look ridiculous with him."

There's nothing like a child when you're looking for brutal honestly. Except I'm not. I'm not looking for any sort of honesty or judgment, from anyone. Least of all from my son. There isn't anything more going on, and Mason is being a friend. But I know he wants something more. I see it. I feel it. He implied it. I want more too. Am I crazy?

I stretch and yawn. "Don't stay up too late. You're going to school in the morning, and no, I'm not driving you so you could be seen in a cool car."

"Aww," Logan groans, as I head to my bedroom.

I drop onto my bed exhausted, but I know I won't be able to close my eyes and allow sleep to whisk me away. Instead, I see a beautiful set of blue eyes burning as they look back at me. His full lips close in on mine. I imagine the passion in his promised kiss igniting sparks in the area surrounding us. My hand ghosts over the skin of my belly. Up, and down, and around my stomach, creeping lower.

Even though I imagine it's Mason touching me, my body knows better. I don't feel the same heat and tingles when I touch myself as I do when he touches me. The same fire burning deep in my belly.

Maybe the reason I can't stop thinking about him, don't wan't to stop thinking about him, is because I'm in need of sex. A *real* physical release. Like hot sweaty flesh on top of hot sweaty flesh.

It's entirely possible that my body craves attention and my heart's getting confused in the turmoil. After all, I've been living like a nun since Keith died. We had a very healthy sex life. We had sex often and tried new things. New places. New positions. New sensations. We learned to take our already good sex to amazing status. For both of us.

And then I stopped cold turkey.

My skin goose fleshes as my fingers creep just below the waistband of my panties. I can't do this. I reach for a pillow and hug it close to my body.

As if he knows I'm thinking about him, my phone chimes with a text message. I hope it's Mason. I want it to be him. My heart thumps with excitement. I waste no time reaching for my phone. *It is him!* I want to jump up and down on the bed in celebration.

Mason: Want to know a secret?

Me: Depends. Is it juicy?

Dots appear. He's typing but it isn't fast enough. I sit up in bed and stare at the screen eager for his response. I'm too excited. Too intrigued. I feel like a five year old promised an ice-cream sundae if I behave.

Mason: I didn't throw Logan in my car and race to you just because he was upset.

I cover my mouth and suck my lips into a thin line between my teeth. He's waiting for a response. I need to say something, but what? I tap my finger on the screen, thinking.

Me: Why did you bring him?

It's lame, but I can't think of anything better and I don't want to keep him hanging for too long. My hands tremble while I wait for his response. The dots start and stop several Times before his message comes across.

Mason: I was worried and needed to see for myself that you were okay.

Me: Needed to?

Mason: Yes. Or else I'd worry when I didn't see you that you were hurt and not just avoiding me.

Oh shit. I can't believe he knows what I've been doing and called me on it. And still, he's been so nice to me.

Me: Why would I avoid you?

Mason: Could be a lot of reasons so I'm not taking it personally. Yet. I guess the question is now that you *know* I want you, are you going to keep hiding or meet me half way?

My chest feels heavy with my heart pounding like a sledge hammer as I read and reread his text. He wants me. Thank goodness he's not here to see the big-ass smile covering my face.

Me: Are you calling me a coward?

Mason: If I am are you ready to prove me wrong?

I hesitate while trying to catch my breath. It comes quick, along with my racing pulse.

Me: I tried meeting you half way earlier. You were the one that chickened out.

Mason: Chickened out, huh? You know what that comment is going to get you?

Me: What?

Mason: Swept into my arms and kissed all over.

Me: You wouldn't.

Mason: Is that a challenge?

Me: Is that all you're going to do? Prove your dominance by holding me hostage while you kiss me?

Mason: Once I have you were I want you, you'll be at my mercy. And I think in your case, being merciful means helping you give in to every feeling and desire you're afraid to let yourself feel.

Me: You're that sure of yourself?

Mason: Yes. And I'm sure of you, too. We'll be good together. I promise.

He *is* pursuing me. There's no more doubt, and it feels amazing. More and more he's invading my thoughts, and continues to thaw my frozen heart. I already feel things I'm afraid to feel, and they aren't just the sexual desires I'm rediscovering. They're actual feelings.

Like the excited anticipation of seeing someone that makes me feel beautiful and relevant in a world I thought forgot me. It's the fact that he's reaching in with his strong hands and yanking me out of the black hole of loneliness and sorrow that sucked me down and suffocated me for the last two years. It's the fact that for the first time since my husband died, I can look at a blue sky and feel hope instead of resentment that somewhere out there someone is falling in love.

Mason: You're awfully quiet. Did I lose you?

Me: You wish.

Mason: I don't want to lose you. I want to catch you and wrap you up in my arms.

I melt a little more with every word he types.

Mason: Where are you right now?

Me: Home, where you left me. :-)

Mason: Wise ass. Where in your house?

Me: In bed.

Mason: Are you thinking about that kiss like I told you to?

Oh. My. Goodness. I think I'm going to spontaneously combust. I take a deep breath.

Me: Maybe.

Mason: I told you one of my secrets, now it's your turn.

Me: I don't have any secrets.

Mason: I call bullshit. I see mischief hidden in those beautiful caramel eyes.

He thinks my eyes are beautiful. The man needs to look in the mirror.

Me: You think you know me that well?

Mason: Not yet. But I want to.

My heart thrums. I know I should question it, ask why, but at the moment, I don't care why. I only care that he wants to.

Mason: Where are your hands?

I hesitate, nervous and excited to take the conversation in this direction.

Me: I'm using the fingers on one hand, moving them back and forth and all around the screen, while the other is holding on tight to my phone.

Mason: Too bad. I was hoping they were moving over your hot body.

Me: What if they are? Or were before you texted me.

Mason: Then I hope you were thinking of me.

Me: What are you going to do once you have me in your arms?

Mason: Is anything off the table?

I hesitate. This is the most difficult word to type.

Me: No.

Mason: Then close your eyes and imagine it. Fantasize about what you want me to do. How you want me to touch you. Where you want me to kiss you. Everywhere you want to feel me.

Is it me or is the phone fifty degrees hotter than it was when we started texting?

Me: Where are your hands?

Mason: I'm using one to type and drink my beer.

Me: And the other?

Mason: Touching myself the way I wish you were touching me right now. With long slow strokes . . . Through my hair.

I laugh.

Me: I had no idea you wanted me that way.

Mason: Then you'll be surprised to learn every way I want you.

Me: Do tell.

Mason: Nah, it will be much more fun showing you.

Me: I really don't know how to thank you. For everything.

Mason: I'm sure we'll come up with something :-).

Me: I have a confession. Before you texted me, I was thinking of you and fighting the urge to touch myself.

I'm thankful he can't see me. My face is on fire, burning with embarrassment.

Mason: If it makes you feel better, I'm doing the same. Now get some sleep. And have sweet dreams of my hands all over your body.

Me: I'll do my best.

I hold my phone clenched close to my chest for the next fifteen minutes, playing with the idea of messaging him again. That give and take was fun. I want more of it. More joking and teasing. More promises of what's going to come. Really I just want more of Mason any way I can get him.

Chapter 10

Beep. Beep. Beep.

The timer sounds. I slip my heat resistant gloves on and open the oven door. Careful not to burn myself, I lean in and pull the tray of freshly baked oatmeal cookies out. They're a perfect golden shade. The sweet smell fills the kitchen. It's a smell I miss wafting through the house for no reason other than I feel like baking. I wonder if the scent made its way to the backyard.

Mason is making good on his offer from a few nights ago to work with Logan, they're focusing on serves and sprawls. Mason brought over a net and set it up in the backyard so Logan has the opportunity to work whenever he wants.

They've been going at it non-stop for the last forty-five minutes. I don't know how much longer they'll be working, but with each passing minute, my face gets hotter and my heart beats faster because I know I'm that much closer to sneaking a few minutes with Mason.

"Go hit the shower," Mason's voice carries into the kitchen as the sliding glass door leading to the back yard opens. I look down trying to hide the smile drawing on my lips.

He's on his way in. I'm celebrating on the inside, giddy as a million dollar lottery winner. I look for some way to busy my nervous hands, and transfer the cookies into a plastic container so I don't look like I'm waiting with baited breath to talk to him, even though that's exactly what I'm doing.

"Those smell delicious. Almost as good as you." Mason whispers into my ear. His warm breath tickles as he cages me in from behind by gripping the counter on either side of me.

He's not touching me. Not with his hands, but his words and the heat of his body caress me, stroke something inside me. Stoke the embers of a very dull flame that he's bringing back to life. A warm shiver races up my spine.

"Want one?" I turn around, with a cookie in hand, not prepared for how close he is. I feel his strength, his energy just from our proximity. We're much closer than we've ever been. Face to face. Chest to chest. Even when I thought he might kiss me for the first time, more air and space existed between us.

"I'd love one," he says, his voice smooth and confident, with his dirty blond hair falling in his face and his blue eyes glued on mine. He takes my wrist and leads my hand to his mouth so I could feed him the sweet treat.

"Mason!" I scold with a smile. "Logan's in the other room."

"He's in the shower. I hear the water running." Mason takes a bite then removes the cookie from my hand while still gripping my wrist. "This is delicious." He slips the tips of my fingers into his mouth gently sucking any crumbs off me. "It's soft, and sweet." He adds circling his skilled tongue around my fingers. "The perfect consistency." Still holding my hand to his mouth, he closes his eyes as he sucks on my fingertips one last time, giving them a final massage with his tongue before releasing his grip on me. "Best damn cookie I ever had."

I can't speak. I'm too focused on his mouth and tongue and the low burning fire throughout my body, most especially between my legs where it seems to have settled. Baking these cookies is the best damn thing I could've done with my free time this morning.

Keith always liked when I surprised him with a tray of warm, home baked cookies. These were his favorite. They're everyone's favorite. I didn't make them today out of some sort of allegiance to my husband. Not out of guilt or because I wanted to keep Keith's memory close at hand. I baked them to do something nice for Mason. Just for Mason.

"You good?" He asks.

My lips curl at the corners as I nod in response. "Never better."

"I don't believe you, but I like the sound of that."

There's been a change in me since the car was stolen. A big one. It's like I woke that night and found I've been living in a cave of darkness. I stayed there, trapped, only I couldn't see it until Mason peeked his head in and found me. He reached in and pulled me from the cold and darkness.

I'm ready to start living again. It's an effort, but I want to give it a go. Even just in small doses. I'm done hiding. I like the excitement Mason riles up in me. The way my heart beats and thrums with thoughts of him. How my whole body responds to the little things he does.

The last few days I've made a point of going inside the school to meet Logan at the end of practice. Mason and I don't speak in public, don't say more than hello and share a cordial smile, but this way I get to see him and catch the heat in his eyes when they land on me.

The nights though, that's where the fun starts. I spend all day looking forward to the dirty words that fly across the screen when I'm alone in bed. Usually around ten o'clock, the texts start up. I make a point to say goodnight to my son and sit in my room, lights dim, with nothing but a bra and underwear on.

I feel pretty and sexy, and it's easier to talk to Mason this way. Easier for me to flirt over text messages. I'm vulnerable but don't feel completely exposed. The interactions are light and playful, and I don't have to worry about getting disoriented by staring in his ocean of blue.

At least the cookies give me an excuse to keep him here for a few extra minutes during daylight hours while I'm fully dressed, and doing something productive. It's a success. I wanted face to face time where we could speak without any jealous mothers or overly hormonal pre-teen boys adding their perverse interpretation to our interaction.

Here I have only to worry about one set of spying eyes. Logan's.

"Hey, Mom." Logan bounds into the kitchen. "I just got a text from Kyle, he invited the team to a sleepover tonight."

"I don't know. I mean I don't really know him or his parents. I'd have to speak to them to make sure it's really okay and that there's going to be parental supervision."

"Yeah, he said his mother will answer any questions. It's just going to be the team and his parents are going to be there. And Zach's going. Please mom, we don't have anything planned. And I heard Mr. Archer talking to Kyle's mom yesterday. He said something like this will help us bond as a team."

I feel a spike in my stomach. A quick sharp jab I have no right to feel.

I keep my eyes off Mason, wondering what really prompted this. "I don't know, honey. I need some time to think about it."

"Fine." Logan storms back off in the direction of his bedroom.

I turn my pointed stare on Mason, sure he manipulated the situation. I'm just not sure why. "You're the one responsible for the imminent sleepover tonight?"

Mason's eyes smolder as they lock on mine. "What can I say? I threw the suggestion out, and Mrs. Stevens ate it up."

Mrs. Stevens? *Mrs. Elaina Stevens who wants to find and follow Mason in a back alley and jump him five ways to Sunday?* My stomach roils. I don't like this feeling. It's foreign, and I haven't felt it in years.

"You didn't just throw it out there, you did it on purpose. You knew she'd take the bait," I say with a sarcastic smirk, hoping to get a clue as to what game he's playing.

"I want alone time with you, and I don't know how to get it." He ignores my implications. "I don't think you're about to leave Logan home alone, and I get it. I'll never ask you to compromise your motherly duties." He slips his arm around my waist, reaches for my hand, and pulls me up against his body, crushes me against his broad chest as he spins us around in a silent dance. "Come out with me tonight. We'll do whatever you want."

"Mason, stop. What if Logan sees," I push at his chest which goes against every instinct and desire I have at the moment.

"Say, yes, and I'll stop." The strength of Mason's strong thigh makes its way between my legs as he bends me backwards in a dip. I grip onto his shoulders and hold on tight to the cords of lean muscle beneath my fingers.

"I never said I wouldn't."

"You never said you would." He keeps me down in the compromised position using the strength of his arms to hold me in place.

"Mason!" I whisper shout sliding my hands up his shoulders and clasping them behind his neck.

"You want up? You know what you need to say. It's just one little word. Just say, yes. It's that simple. That easy. Or else Logan will have a lot of questions when he sees you like this."

"You can't keep me like this forever," I tease.

"Long enough. You're very light, so I can hold you like this for a long time. Besides, it's not like I mind being this close to you. Having your undivided attention on me. Feeling the heat build between your legs."

He moves the thigh between my legs, pressing it against my center, adding pressure, making me want to feel more there. It's hard for me to say anything, least of all no. He pulls everything out of his bag of tricks to wear me down, and it's working.

"You'll have a good time. I promise."

"Fine! Yes! You win. I'll go out with you tonight!"

"By the way, saying yes doesn't mean I win. It means we both win."

*

I take a deep breath before pulling the black pencil across the length of my bottom lid. My hair is in a diagonal twist that starts on the left side of my head and ends over my right shoulder. I stand in front of the full length mirror, turning side to side to see myself from different angles. Pleased with my reflection I head to the living room to wait for my date.

My date!

I still can't believe Mason asked me out on an actual date.

Asked, that's funny. More like he bullied me. Not that I mind the kind of pressure he applied. Or that I said yes. I wanted to say yes, he just gave me a guilt free excuse to. I have mixed emotions about the whole thing, but I want to see where tonight goes. I'm ready to start living again, and I can't think of a better way to jumpstart this new phase of my life than a date with Mason Archer.

The doorbell rings. I bounce up and down in place before moving to the door. It's hard to find the balance between being excited and not giving a shit. I want to appear somewhere in the middle. It's hard though, because on the other side of my front door is a man that sends my body into hyper drive.

Fear and excitement are rolled up into one large, hot, sexy ball of the forbidden and unknown. By the end of the night, I'm hoping to have a taste of the fruit that will lead me straight out of garden of ignorance.

Chapter 11

The third kamikaze of the night makes my head feel like a giant glass of champagne; bubbles effervesce, float to the top and pop. My thoughts are fizzy and revolve around Mason. Every few minutes I lose myself in thoughts of his mouth on mine, of ripping his shirt off and running my hands over his sculpted chest while pressing up against him.

It takes all my willpower to fight off these thoughts. Once I'm pulled back to the present, my brain gets fuzzy and the process starts all over again. Bubble. Pop. Fizz.

I look at Mason, and cover my mouth with my hand to hide a nervous giggle from escaping. I can't help it. When I look at him I'm no different than the pre-teen girls he deals with at school. He must fill out a lot of accident reports, because I can't imagine the girls can focus on the games being played in phys ed while he's in the vicinity.

The atmosphere of the restaurant/sports bar encourages my giddy behavior. People laugh and have a good time around us. I stay in the moment, let go and laugh. At everything. Every silly and sexy comment Mason makes when I lean over the Billiard table to try and make a shot brings a smile to my face.

After doing nothing more than spraying the balls across the felt, I head over to the table on the side where Mason takes a long pull of his beer. As I approach he reaches his hand out and takes mine. I like how I feel when he touches me. Sexy. Sultry.

He rubs his calloused thumb over the soft skin on the back of my hand and the friction crackles and sparks deep in my lower valley. I squeeze my thighs together hoping that will alleviate the all-consuming ache I have between my legs when I'm near him. The ache that's had me exploring and touching myself when I text with him at night in search of satisfaction. Satisfaction I haven't been able to find.

God, do I want him.

"How do you feel?" He whispers. A cocky, self-assured smirk plays on his pouty lips. Lips I imagine all over my body.

Inappropriate responses I'm not about to admit race through my head. *Horny. Turned on. Desperate.*

"I'm feeling . . . Good."

"Just good?" He steps forward closing the distance. His blue eyes are so hot I almost see steam coming out of them. "You look gorgeous." His eyes drop from my face and inch down to my chest. They linger there while the color of his eyes deepens. Darkens.

He cocks one eyebrow as he stares at my breasts. I feel my nipples come to life and tighten under his scrutiny. Mason doesn't bother trying to hide his thoughts, I don't want him to. I'm not used to a man looking at me with lust in his eyes and I like it.

He shakes his head, "I don't know if I'm going to be able to keep my hands off you until we get home."

A low purr forms in my throat as I openly ogle the man standing inches away from me. I'd like to blame the alcohol for my wandering mind. It keeps ripping his dark, tight fitting shirt over his head so I can touch his pecs. Kiss him. Lick him. I want to run my hands all over his body.

"Thank you. For whatever strings you pulled to make this happen. Even if you did promise Mrs. Stevens an hour alone behind the school." I hiccup.

Mason squeezes my hand and laughs. The sound is infectious. I want to hear more of it.

"You're not implying I traded sex for favors with her are you?"

I shrug. "I think that's sort of her plan. She wants you."

"Oh yeah?" He pauses a beat and then comes right at me. "How about you? Do you want me?"

"You already know the answer to that." My teeth scrape over my bottom lip as I shift from leg to leg uncomfortable with the pulsing down below.

"I want you to say it. To me. Not over text."

I look at Mason through my lashes inviting him to take me. To have his way with me. I pause for dramatic effect, licking my lip before I answer. "Very much."

"Shit, Ambs. What do you say we leave right now?"

"Patience," I tease, reaching for my drink and eyeing him as I wrap my lips around the thin plastic straw and pull a long sip from it. He's captivated, and I feel an internal pride at holding his attention so completely. "Patience is a virtue."

"Is that what you want? For me to be virtuous?"

I shake my head, feeling the bubbles shift from side to side. "No. But the foreplay will make the main event that much better."

Mason reaches around me and I feel his hands on the back of my thighs. I close my eyes and take a long pull of air savoring his touch. Content and enamored with my date, I'm barely aware of the crowd around us. Until a loud brash voice breaks through.

"Oh my God. Look at them." I don't look away from Mason, but I feel eyes, lots of curious, judgmental eyes crawling over me. "Fully grown and he's still cuddling with his mommy."

Sober from the laughter that follows, I put distance between Mason and me.

"Do you blame him?" Another male voice rings out. "I mean, look at those tits. If she were my mother, I'd still be breastfeeding, too."

My heart hammers against my chest, and heat fills my face. I'm embarrassed. Mortified by the raucous laughter around us. I don't dare look around, but keep my eyes on the man in front of me everyone is laughing. I hear it. I feel it. And they are laughing at me. I work to pull my hand from Mason's grip, but he doesn't let me.

"What do you say, mama?" A man from the rowdy group calls to me. "Want to adopt another son? I want to suck on those big titties, too. And I promise to be bad so you could take me over your knee and spank me."

I hear Logan's voice in my head, telling me how ridiculous I look with Mason. My son tried to warn me, and I ignored him. It's difficult to breathe. Without a word to Mason, I reach for my purse and head for the exit. Once outside, I scrub my hands up and down over my face. I'm an idiot. I never should've allowed myself to get caught up in the fantasy of being with him. I'm supposed to know better. I'm forty three, not twenty three.

"Hey." Mason catches up after a minute and stands in front of me. He looks pale. Frightened. "Those guys are jackasses."

I don't speak, I only stare.

"Don't take it personally."

"Take what personally, that I'm the butt of a joke? That me being with you, that this," I point back and forth between us. "Is something for the rest of the world to mock and laugh at? Is that what I'm not supposed to take personally?"

"I don't care about the rest of the world. Let them laugh. Does it really matter?"

"Yes, It matters."

"Why?"

"Because we look ridiculous together."

"No, baby." He strokes the side of my face with the back of his fingers. "We look good together. We look really good together."

"That's why they took one look at us and ridiculed me?"

"Yes. Maybe this was exactly the reaction they hoped for. That you'd walk away from me, and that would leave an opening for them. Amber, you don't see what I see when I look at you. What every other man sees. You're beautiful, and sexy as hell."

I shake my head. "And old."

"You're not old. Besides, who gives a fuck what other people think? You shouldn't give a shit about anyone but you and me."

"Oh, god." I turn, cross my arms over my chest and take a few long strides away from him. There's nowhere to go except for around the building, toward the parking lot in the back. With limited choices, I turn and head down the side of the building. As long as it gets me further from the entrance of the pub, and away from Mason, it's where I want to be.

"Don't do this, Amber." Mason grabs my elbow, stopping me. He turns me around to face him again. "Don't punish me because of those asshats."

"Punish you? Really? The whole place laughed at *me*, and you think you're the one that's being punished?"

It's darker on this side of the building. I can't see the features of Mason's face clearly, which I think is a blessing until I realize the moonlight illuminating his silhouette increases his sex appeal tenfold. My breath catches in the back of my throat. I remind myself it doesn't matter how attracted to him I am I can't let things go any further.

"I'm sorry, Mason. I don't know what you were hoping for, but I can't give it to you."

"Bullshit." He inches toward me in the dark. Slow. Seductive. Like he's a hunter and I'm his prey.

The moonlight casts a silver lining around Mason as he cups my face in his hands. He advances while I retreat. My back hits the wall behind me, still he moves closer. Closer. Until he cages me between him and the concrete.

It's hard to swallow. My pulse races. There's a lump in the back of my throat. Mason's chest presses against mine. My breasts brush against him with each breath of air. I arc my back toward him and lay my hand on his cheek. Mason turns his head, his soft lips caress my palm. My heart thunders. In protest. In angst. In excitement.

Mason skims his thumbs over my cheeks. Back and forth, while his eyes search mine in the dark. Even in this muted light, I can see the resolve, the determination in his eyes. I want to listen, to believe that the rest of the world doesn't matter, and fall into him.

"You're afraid," he whispers. "That's all this is. You're afraid of getting hurt."

"No—"

"Yes," he insists, taking my hand and placing it on his chest. He moves our joined hands over his own pounding heart. "I'm just as nervous, just as excited as you."

I don't pull away, but shake my head.

The pointer finger of Mason's other hand glides over the neck line of my shirt. All I want is for him to slip his fingers, his whole hand inside and brush it along my tightened buds.

"Tell me you don't want this." His mouth is next to my ear, his warm breath makes me shiver. "Tell me you don't want me to touch you," he whispers, using that same finger to trace over my lips. "That right now, you're not imagining my mouth on yours.

"Mason, don't—"

"Shh."

It's all the warning I get before he snakes his arm around the small of my back and crushes me tight against him. His hand slides down and cups my backside. I clasp my hands around his neck and whimper as his free hand urges my head forward. His lips inch toward me. Slow. So achingly slow.

I want this to happen. I want it more than I'm afraid for it. I fist the back of his shirt in my hands and hold on tight as Mason's warm lips meet mine. Soft, powerful lips. His tongue swipes across my mouth until I open up and let him in.

I kiss him back hungry. Eager. Until I can't breathe. Until kissing him is all that there is, all that's right with the world. I take in a deep breath before Mason bombards me again. His tongue brushes against mine. It twists and twirls, deepening the kiss. I'm hungry, dizzy with need.

I forget that we're outside in public. The night air is like an aphrodisiac I don't care that we're making a spectacle of ourselves as Mason lifts me up by the back of my thighs. My legs wrap around his waist. My long skirt rides up and a thin scrap of lace is the only barrier keeping my pleasure zone protected.

Mason squeezes my flesh. He peppers a trail of searing kisses along my throat, across my chest. His hips press and rock into me. Grind against me. Soak my panties with desire. I wonder if he could feel through his jeans how wet and ready I am.

Carnal sounds leave Mason as he continues to simulate having sex with me against the side of the building. He presses his bulge against my warm, aching center, rubbing it against me. I moan, breathing heavy. Wanting more. Needing more.

"Tell me you don't want this." His voice is rough. Gravelly. "That you're not imagining me inside you," He whispers, then nips on my shoulder.

I can't. I can't say anything. If I could, I'd be begging, pleading for him to take me here. Now.

"Tell me your body's not humming with need."

"Mason . . ." I manage to get out.

He moans and closes his eyes at the sound of his name. I could almost cum in this moment, just by looking at his face. His eyes open, and even through the lack of light, I can see the lust shining through.

"I want you, Amber. So fucking bad." My name slides off his lips, and it's the most beautiful sound. "I want to take you home and bury myself deep inside you."

"Mason," I can barely get the words out. "Take me home."

He exhales hard and sets me on my feet. "And then what?"

"And then . . . Have your way with me."

Chapter 12

Strong arms wrap around me and hold me close. I lean back and snuggle against Mason's bare chest, inhaling his familiar scent of sandalwood mixed with sex.

"Good morning, beautiful." He hooks his leg over mine.

"Morning."

"Sorry I didn't let you get much sleep." His chest vibrates as he speaks.

My mind flashes back to the previous night.

Mason's front door closes. His hands slide over my hips and lift my skirt. His hungry mouth trails down my neck. With his hand on my lower back he pulls me against him and lowers the zipper of my skirt. He tosses the black fabric to the floor. In a quick swift movement, he lifts my shirt and discards it.

Mason takes a moment to let his heated stare run over me in my favorite bra and panty set. Reaching behind me, Mason unhooks the bra and slides the straps down my arms. He fills each hand with a breast. His broad chest heaves as his mouth meets mine. I grab at his shirt with the same hunger and desperation he has for me.

"Sleep is overrated. I'll take a night like last night over sleep anytime."

His calloused thumb brushes over and perks up my nipple. "I hope that's an invitation for more nights together." He nips my shoulder. Sending a wave of heat down to the top of my thighs "Many, many more."

Mason's lips caress my nipples, wrapping around each in turn. He nibbles and licks before sucking. His hand reaches between my legs. His fingers slide over my damp skin, working their way to the little bundle of nerves.

I pull his shirt over his head then rest my hands on his chest. His heart thumps beneath my fingers. He's warm and hard with dips and creases carving out each bunch of muscles. He looks even better than I imagined. I trace the peaks and valleys as my fingers glide down his center. Down his naval to the button of his pants.

Mason plunges his fingers inside me. Watching me with a lustful stare. Hot. Burning.

I close my eyes and revel in every sensation he's bringing to the surface. I want him to see the pleasure on my face. I want to be worthy of his attention.

"You're so tight. So warm and welcoming. And deliciously tight."

His tongue works its way into my mouth again. Brushing and stroking mine. His fingers stroke and thrust inside me. Slow then hard. In and out. I grip his hardened length. He's long and thick and I want him inside me.

For every action I take, Mason pushes further. Harder. His fingers delve deeper. Mason kisses me passionately while his thumb circles my hardening clit.

I look at his glorious body as I push his pants and underwear down.

"You're very quiet." He holds me tighter.

"I'm thinking."

"About?"

"Last night."

He peppers a trail of hot kisses along the crook of my neck. I moan in response.

"Mmm. I love the sounds you make."

I turn in his arms so I can face him, reach between his legs and stroke his hardness. Mason's eyes close. I run my tongue and lips down his chest, down his abdomen, all the way down. I bring my mouth to his tip and swirl it over the top, licking the precum.

I hallow out my cheeks and slide my mouth down his cock. The guttural sounds of pleasure leaving Mason spur me on.

My hand reaches for his balls. Stumped, I stop, hesitate for a split second before I force myself back in the moment, back to the task at hand and massage. I noticed it was there last night. Rather, that it wasn't there. It doesn't matter. Using my other hand I pump the base of his cock while I lick it up and down.

Mason threads his fingers through my hair and tugs lightly. I drag my tongue up the thick vein running the length of his shaft and devour his head when I reach the top. I suck harder.

"Fuck, Amber!"

I pull my mouth off him for a second and look at the god I'm pleasing through my lashes. In this moment if he weren't laying on his back, I think I'd bring him to his knees. In a heartbeat, he pounces on me, flips me on my back and climbs on top.

"You like teasing me?"

I offer him a salacious smile. "Very much."

"Oh yeah?" I see a hint of humor in his eyes, hidden behind the heat of his stare.

Taking hold of my ankles, Mason bends my knees up on either side of my chest. He stops and looks at me, eyes hooded, mouth open as he slips his shaft inside me. He moves slow, inch by inch, allowing me to once again stretch and adjust to his size before he picks up force and speed.

I'm vaguely aware that he's not wearing anything. Unlike last night when we used a condom. We used a whole box of condoms. This is stupid, I know. It's a risk I shouldn't take, but something about it feels . . . right.

It's not like I'm going to get pregnant. I've already started going through my changes. I haven't had my period for three months now. Sure it's early, but who's going to argue with nature?

Mason keeps his eyes glued on mine. He rests his weight on his muscular forearms, sweat beads form as he continues to drive me to new heights. Plunging inside me, we climb higher and higher. We arrive at the peak of pleasure at the same time. I see it in his face as he fights to hold back until my body goes limp beneath him.

Mason pulls out and cums on my stomach.

"Sorry. I should've asked first. I'm out of condoms, and I swear I'm clean."

I nod. "It's fine. Me too."

He chuckles. "I sort of had a feeling you are."

"Besides, I don't have to worry about getting pregnant."

"Then that makes life much more interesting." He smiles, and his eyes are full of mischief as he rubs his warm seed over my belly and breasts.

"Are you marking me?"

"That's exactly what I'm doing."

When he's satisfied with his work, Mason holds my head against his chest, smoothing my hair while he catches his breath.

"Is there something you want to ask me?"

I shake my head. I know what he's referring to, but I can't ask. It's too personal. And he has an amazing body. It obviously doesn't interfere with performance. Do I want him to think a little imperfection bothers me? It doesn't. Although I am curious.

"Testicular cancer," he offers as if he can read my mind.

I move over, lie on my side and push myself up so that I'm leaning on my arm facing him. "I don't know what you're talking about."

"So you didn't notice that I have a uni-ball."

Heat fills my face. I tried to play it off. I did my best to hide any reaction when I cupped his balls. Correction, ball.

"It's not that I noticed. It's just kind of hard not to."

He laughs and strokes my hair. "It's fine. I would've told you, but I don't know how to casually bring it up in conversation. Especially since it assumes a lot."

"You don't have to talk about it."

"It's okay. I want to. It's a part of who I am. Everything we go through, every challenge, every triumph, shapes who we are."

A bright light goes off above my head. "That's how you know. How you understand me so well."

He nods. "Yes. I know what it's like to go through the worst time of your life. And I'm proof that it's possible to come back from it and be happy. That was my lowest point.

I was nineteen, and thought I was invincible. It sure as hell wasn't anything I ever thought I'd have to deal with."

I cup his cheek. "Aww, Mason. I'm so sorry. Especially since you were so young."

He shrugs and looks away. "You don't get to choose when these things happen. You know that." He kisses the top of my head. "Besides, there's no good time for your life to be scorched to the ground. You just have to play the hand you're dealt."

I can't believe how rational, how well adjusted he sounds. *Isn't he angry?* I know I'd be. Hell I am angry. I'm angry at the prick that killed Keith. Angry at Keith for dying. Angry at the damn universe for taking away the love of my life.

Only lately, I've been less angry. And the pain hasn't felt as sharp or deep. I still miss Keith like crazy, but since Mason entered the picture, I feel lighter. Brighter. I'm starting to enjoy things, like seeing and texting with him.

"Still, it couldn't have been easy," I say, trying to hide how choked up I am.

"It wasn't. I just started college. I loved being away at school, and then my whole life changed. I had to take a medical leave for the semester. Things got worse after the surgery. It destroyed the relationship with my girlfriend."

Girlfriend. It's the first time I heard anything about someone special in his life past or present. There are so many questions I want to ask, but I don't know if they would come across as nosy, or cold and callous.

"Serious girlfriend?"

"Yeah." He pushes up to a sitting position. Holding the covers over my breasts, I sit and sidle up next to him. I can only guess this is a difficult subject and I want to lend him whatever support and comfort I can.

"Ashley." I hear the reverence of her name in the way he says it. "She was my high school sweetheart. We'd been together for two years already. We went to college together and practically lived with each other since we were housed in the same dorm. She'd sleep in my room, or I'd spend the night in hers. We loved being together and waking up in each other's arms. Then I got the diagnosis and I wasn't there. Everything changed."

"You were going through all this and she broke up with you?"

"No." He smiles, but it's a sad smile. "She'd never do that. She didn't want to hurt me. But she didn't know what to say or how to act around me. Things felt forced. They never were before. She was just . . . different. Distant. We couldn't relate to each other anymore. That was the hardest part, because even though we were young, I loved her. I thought she was the one. We often spoke about our future, and planned to move in together after graduation so we could save up to get married."

"Wow. What happened?"

"She hooked up with my roommate." His eyes drop, as he speaks. "A couple of weeks after I finished chemo, I felt good, and I wanted to surprise her. I didn't tell her I was coming to visit. I couldn't find her. She wasn't in her room, so I went to say hi to the guys on my floor. No one expected me, so neither of them saw me standing only feet away. My heart dropped when I saw them tangled up in each other's arms. Kissing. I wanted to die. For a very brief time, I wished the cancer spread and was undetectable."

Tears pool in my eyes and blur my vision. I have no reason to feel such a strong connection to Mason, but the thought of death stealing him too, it slices me to the core.

"Don't say that. Please."

I lean in and kiss his cheek. His warm, stubble covered, very alive cheek. My heart, heavy with emotion, thunders against my chest. I'm not sure if it's from the thought of someone hurting this godsend of a man, or fear of something awful stealing him from the world.

"Hey," he brushes the lone tear that falls from my eye away with the pad of his thumb. "I'm fine, Ambs. I've healed. All of me. And I moved on."

"I'm sorry," I sniffle. "I don't mean to overreact. It's just I can't stand the thought of something happening to you . . ."

"Fuck." He runs his hand through his hair. "Sorry. I'm an ass. I never should've said that."

"No. I want you to be honest. But the thought of something happening to you . . . I know we're not . . ."

I don't get to finish my thought before his mouth covers mine, shutting me up. This kiss is soft and gentle. He pulls me close as he slides down in the bed pulling me on top of him. His hand moves in small circles on my back, while his tongue twirls in unison with mine. This kiss is different than the others we shared. It's sweet and emotional, and sends me spiraling into the stratosphere.

"Just so you know, I wouldn't change anything that happened in my life. Because everything has lead up to what's happening here and now. And as far as she's concerned, it was better to know sooner rather than later that we weren't right for each other. Before we had kids and managed to screw up their lives with a divorce, or an unhappy marriage."

"You like where you're at?"

"If you mean in bed with you? Abso-fucking-lutely!" He nuzzles my neck, and at the moment I like where I am too. I like it so much, I think if the world would let me, I'd be happy to stay here forever.

Chapter 13

I open the file for the current manuscript I'm editing. It's an author I've worked with before. I really like her style. Her writing keeps me engaged, and she's unpredictable. She packs the pages with twists and turns I don't see coming.

The ringing of my phone pulls me from the confrontation between the bad boy billionaire and his feisty step-sister. Running for her life because she witnessed a murder, she asks him to hide her in his tropical island home. The sexual tension has been building and I think things are about to cross familial lines. I check the caller ID and my pulse ticks up a notch.

It's Mason. He's redefined what I know about sexual tension. I'm surprised, and excited to speak to him. He doesn't usually call during the school day.

"Hey sexy."

Even over the phone his velvety voice turns me into a puddle. My mind races back to the manuscript I'm reading, only the characters running through my head are no longer the ones the author wrote, they've morphed into Mason and me dripping with water on a white beach, surrounded by a crystal blue ocean.

"Hey, yourself. What can I do for you?"

"As I'm in a public setting I'll save that for tonight. I know we had plans to go shopping."

"You mean for a new car?"

"Yes."

"It's fine if you can't make it." I hope to hide my disappointment. "I thought since I know next to nothing about cars—"

"I'm not backing out."

"Oh." I hate how relieved I feel. "Then what's up?"

"I got a request from a mutual friend, and I said, yes."

Mutual friend? There must be someone around that he doesn't want to pick up on what or who he's talking about. There's only one person we share a relationship with. Unless he's talking about Elaina Stevens. I hate to even think of the type of request she'd have for him. She'd probably beg him to have sex with her in his Mustang. I seriously hope she's not the one he's talking about.

"Logan?"

"Um hum."

"What kind of request?"

"He'd like to use it to impress a certain lady friend."

"Lady Friend, but he can't even drive."

"No. But you can."

My head spins. I have no idea what Mason is talking about. He can't want me to drive him and Delaney somewhere. Logan still won't talk to me about her, so I can't see that he'd want me to actually meet her.

When I ask questions he gives me as little information as possible then changes the subject. Like I'm not supposed to recognize that tactic. I do drop it though, because the last thing I want is for my son to press me on Mason. I know he likes Mason, but he's not keen on the idea of his coach and I being anything more than friends. He made that perfectly clear.

"Are you going to explain or am I supposed to guess what's going on?" I ask.

He chuckles. "I enjoy frustrating you and working you into a frenzy. Too bad I'm not there to see how cute you look."

"If you want I could send you a selfie, but I think I look annoyed, not cute."

"Do you have plans this afternoon?"

He's working hard not to let on to who he's speaking with. It shouldn't bother me but something about it gnaws at me. I get that we're just . . . I don't know what we are, or what we're doing, but whatever it is, it's not like we're a real couple. We've been sneaking around for the last two weeks.

I know it's what I wanted, and it's about keeping Logan in the dark, but right about now, I'd like to rethink that strategy.

"I'll be at the match if that's what you're asking."

"Good. See you then."

"Dinner after?"

"If you're up for it."

"Absolutely. We'll call it an end of season celebration."

*

All through dinner, the talk is about volleyball. Logan's spent more time on the court, had three service aces, five assists and helped the team win the last game of the season.

"Told you things would turn around if you work hard and believe in yourself."

"Thanks, Mr. Archer." My son's eyes shine with excitement. "It wouldn't have happened without the extra help."

"No problem. I'm happy to do it."

"But the season's over. I'm still not good enough for the high school team."

Mason's eyebrows furrow together. "Are you going to quit working?"

Logan smiles. "No, but, you won't be helping me anymore."

"You planning on sneaking out of here on Saturday mornings?"

Logan shakes his head. "No, sir."

"Well then," Mason looks serious, I'd even go so far as to say with his eyes narrowed and the firm set of his jaw, he looks stern. "We'll continue to work."

"For real?"

"As long as you put in the effort, you can count on help from me."

"Wow. I don't know what to say."

"Do me a favor, and make sure you help your mother around the house. I don't want to hear you give her an attitude, or a hard time. Got it?"

Logan nods. "Yes, sir."

"And I'll pass along some information to your mother about leagues and clubs you can play in over the off season."

"You're the best!"

Hearing my son say this to Mason shouldn't bring tears to my eyes, but it does. Tears of joy. Mason will never take Keith's place in Logan's heart but he's definitely worked his way as a person of trust in Logan's life.

"Was that Delany I saw in the gym?" Mason asks, his voice is much softer.

Logan's eyes drop, and his cheeks take on a pinkish hue. I can't believe my smart mouthed tough guy is actually blushing!

"Yeah." Logan's eyes meet Mason's for a second before they drop back down to the food on his plate. He stabs a piece of roast beef with his fork, stuffs it in his mouth and chews before speaking again. "She wanted to see me play. I hope she saw my aces."

"I don't know how long she was there I really don't pay attention to who's on the sidelines watching." Not true. Mason notices me often enough. "But if she was and she saw you all sweaty and disheveled digging for balls and she still likes you, you've got it made."

"You think?"

"Oh yeah. That's how I could tell which girls were really into me in college."

I bet there were throngs of them.

"At least I asked Delany to go before the game. She hasn't texted to say she changed her mind, so I probably didn't look that stupid." Logan teases back.

"Go where?" I put my fork down and look at my son. He swallows hard. His over active nerves show through his wandering eyes.

"Um, maybe I should've asked you first, Mom." He looks at me, then down at the table before lifting his eyes to Mason's then back to me. "But I didn't think you'd have a problem with me going. I know I don't usually, but it's my last year of middle school, and I thought it might be nice to see what it's like—"

"Spit it out, honey. Where do you want to go?"

His eyes dart over to Mason again. I'm not sure why. For support? Mason's head bobs up and down the slightest bit.

"I asked Delany to go the eighth grade formal with me. And she said yes."

"That's great, Logan." I smile and reach my hand over to his.

He nods, and I see the lump in his throat bob up and down as he swallows.

"I thought maybe we could pick her up, so it really is like we're going together, rather than meeting at school like a lot of the other kids do. And I know you're supposed to go car shopping this weekend, but I asked Mr. Archer if we could pick her up in the Mustang."

Finished with his second helping of food, Mason leans back in his chair with a cocky look on his face.

"Of course I said, yes." Mason leans over and messes Logan's hair up. "Can't have you picking her up on your bicycle."

"Who knows, maybe you'll change your mind after you see the new car?"

Logan scoffs. "C'mon, Mom. It's not like you're going to get anything cool."

That comment bites, because my son is right. I won't get a sports car or something to have fun in. I'll get something safe and practical to transport my son in.

"Obviously nothing cooler than what Mr. Archer has."

"We can work something out where you can keep my car if you'd like, or I can sell it to you at a deep discount."

Keeping Mason's car would insinuate a lot. It would also attach strings to the both of us. Besides, I want something that I can pay off over time to minimize the reduction in my bank account. While a used car would be cheaper, his used car is in excellent shape and worth much more than I'm willing to spend on something that doesn't come with a bumper to bumper warranty.

"Forget it." I respond to Mason, but Logan thinks I'm answering him.

"We can't pick her up in the Mustang? Why not?"

"I kind of already agreed. I mean even if you do find something this weekend, you'll only hold onto my car for an extra week." Mason's chimes in.

"Wait, the dance is next weekend?"

"Next Saturday." Logan answers holding his breath.

"Yeah. Sure. Of course we can pick her up in the Mustang." I smile at my son.

I won't admit it, but I'm secretly happy that Logan will be out that night. It would be nice to have some time alone with Mason. We haven't been able to steal more than an hour here and there together, since the night he convinced Mrs. Steven's to host a sleepover.

A few times I told Logan I'm going to work at a coffee shop to clear my mind. Mason waits with coffee for me in his car. We drive to a secluded spot so we can kiss, touch and grope each other without giving everyone around us a show.

I run recipes through my mind. I'll cook a romantic dinner, and then . . .

"And I'll be able to keep an eye on lover-boy over here," Mason pulls me from my dirty thoughts. "Since I'm one of the chaperones."

"You are?"

My voice rises three octaves. Holy hell, why not just slam a brick in my face. It's my insecurity telltale. Mason won't know for certain, but hopefully neither will Logan.

Mason is chaperoning?

Is he doing that so he has an excuse not to spend that night with me?

Silence fills the room. I don't know if the guys feel the tension in the air, but it weighs me down. Logan finishes the helping on his plate, clears it from the table and places it in the sink before disappearing to his room.

I stand and head to the kitchen to get right to the dishes. I don't want to sit and stare at the man that makes the butterflies soar to life in my belly. And I don't want to be forced to talk to him. I have no idea what the hell to say. All I know is that I'm upset and I have no right to be.

Arms slip around my waist as his warm lips graze the back of my neck, tickling me. He pulls me against his chest, and all I want to do is forget the frosty demeanor I struggle to drape around my heart, and melt into him. I hate that he already knows one of my weaknesses.

"I have to say," his breath tickles my ear. "I never snuck around with any one before. This is so hot."

His hands slide down my legs and cup my ass. I close my eyes and fight to stay in control.

"You need to stop. If Logan comes in here—"

Mason lets go. He leans his back against the counter and crosses his arms over his chest, letting out a long breath. What I just said bothered him. It's not often something I say sends him into a defensive posture.

"We should tell him."

"He'll shut down. He's already so distant. So far away emotionally. Tonight was great. I want more nights like this. I don't want to give him an excuse to pull further away."

"If he finds out he'll feel betrayed. By both of us."

"If you're careful, he won't find out." I insist.

"About the dance—"

"No worries. It's not like I expected to see you." I do my best to play off my disappointment.

I don't want to say or do anything that will imply a relationship. And feelings. Real, strong, serious feelings. Even though I'm there it's wrong to assume he is, even though he started this whole thing. Still, I can't think in those terms or I'm the one that's going to end up hurt. Very hurt.

"Really? Do you have other plans?" he challenges.

"No," I look away, because the deep blue of his eyes is too damn intense. Too damn intimidating. "But it's just another Saturday night."

"That's my point. The school holds four dances a year. We all have to chaperone one. I signed up for this a long time ago. I'd love to switch with someone, but the other dances already happened. At least this way I'll be there for Logan if he needs some moral support or if something goes wrong."

I feel the tiniest bit better.

"You don't owe me an explanation." In truth, he doesn't owe me anything.

"I think I do. You're upset."

"I'm not." I lie.

"Oh yeah? Then why are you standing so far away."

"I'm not far."

"You are."

"I'm a foot away from you."

"Exactly. You're not here. In my arms."

He reaches for me and pulls me close. I let him, because the truth is, his arms are exactly where I want to be.

Chapter 14

"Hurry up, Logan, you don't want to be late!"

"Be right there," my son yells back.

He's been on edge all day. Anyone who heard him while getting his hair cut would think he's going to show up on the red carpet tonight rather than at a middle school dance.

"Don't forget, she'll want to take pictures so you need to plan to get there early."

"How do I look?" Logan comes in wearing a maroon button down shirt, with gray dress pants and a thin gray tie. He wears shoes instead of his usual sneakers, and even though he just had his hair cut earlier in the day, and the back and sides are shaved close to his scalp, he rewashed and styled the top and front so that his hair parts to the side and hangs just above his left eye.

I cover my open mouth with my hand unprepared for this. He looks handsome. That I'm used to, but not like this. This is a mature-I'm-trying-to-impress-girls kind of handsome.

"What? Did I miss-button my shirt?" Logan looks down to check for himself.

"Not at all. You look great."

"I hope she thinks so."

"I'm sure she will."

The doorbell rings. I look around the house. Two laundry baskets full of clean, unfolded clothes sit on the couch. It doesn't look awful, but certainly not the way I want the house to look for company. Especially not for someone who's never been here before.

"Logan, you sure you're supposed to meet at her house?"

"Mom, I know where we're supposed to meet."

"Do you have any idea who's at the door?"

My son shakes his head.

I open the door, and my heart skips a beat. Mason stands in front of me. He's dressed for the dance, in black pants, a sapphire blue button down shirt that deepens the color of his eyes, and a paisley tie.

I think my panties melted in the last thirty seconds.

I never saw him dressed up like this. Usually it's sweats or jeans. A playful light shines in his eyes as they crawl up and down my body. His eyes hold magic because with just that look, my body tingles.

"May I come in for a minute?" He pulls me from my staring stupor.

I look away so I can think and speak clearly. "Of course. Sorry. I wasn't expecting you. Can I get you a drink?"

"No. I'm here to see Logan for a minute."

"Oh." My stomach drops like a rock into a bottomless ocean. I call out to my son.

"Hey, now," Mason wears a sexy, smug look. The one he wears far too often when he knows he has the better of me. "No pouting. I'm doing this the only way I can."

I'm confused, but I step to the side to make way for my son.

"Hey, man, I thought you might want to give this to Delany."

Mason reaches behind his back and hands Logan a red rose. How the hell did he pull that off, I didn't even see it. My heart warms, my eyes tear. Mason is going out of his way for Logan. He's a good man. I feel incredibly lucky that he's in both of our lives.

"Thanks, Mr. Archer. I didn't think of a flower."

"Then I'm betting you didn't think of one for your mother either."

Logan shakes his head. "No, I didn't."

"Then I'm glad I did."

Mason reaches behind his back again and hands my son another red rose. Now I know what he meant. This is the only way he can give me something, anything, without raising Logan's suspicion.

"After all, she'll always be the most important woman in your life."

With this realization comes an even more frightening one. I'm not falling for Mason anymore. The fall started during that first conversation on the school steps months ago. He worked his way under my skin, inch by inch, until he infiltrated my heart. Now I'm done falling. I've landed someplace I never thought possible, and it terrifies me.

"Thanks, Mr. Archer."

"Alright," Mason, claps his hands together. "My job here is done. I need to get to school."

I don't want him to leave. I want to pull him inside and drown him in kisses to show him what's in my heart and how much I appreciate what he did. I can't though. I can't do anything but say thank you and watch him go.

"See you later." Logan's voice pulls me back into the moment. "Mom, I'm going to text Delany and make sure she's ready."

"Thank you," I say, before Mason gets in his car.

He turns back, and the look in his eyes . . . I can't move. I'm frozen. Held in place by his very hot stare.

"It's my pleasure."

*

After taking about a hundred pictures at Delany's house, many with the Mustang as a backdrop, we arrive at school.

Mason was right, I do like Delany. She seems like a very sweet girl. Polite. Well mannered. And very pretty.

It's not hard to see what Logan likes about her. She laughs at his jokes and has a nice sense of humor. This is the type of girl I want Logan to hang around. I couldn't have picked out someone nicer for him.

I don't bother parking. Instead, I pull up in front of the school building like all the other parents and say goodbye as Logan gets out and walks around to open the door for his friend. Friend, that's a joke. Anyone with half decent vision could see he's head over heels for her. Delany's shy, flirty smiles give away her interest in my son.

I watch with pride as the kids enter the school hoping I'll catch a glimpse of Mason. I know I just saw him, but I never get enough of him, no matter how much time we steal away. I always want more.

Unfortunately, he's not outside. I see his car in the parking lot. It's not as good as seeing him, but knowing he's near makes me happy. I leave looking forward to later in the night when we can text.

I go home wondering how I'll pass the two hours I need to kill before I pick the kids up. I pull a vase out of the cabinet and fill it with water. Before putting my rose in, I trim the bottom and add sugar.

I bring the flower to my nose and breathe in the sweet fragrant scent. I love the way Mason maneuvered to give this to me. I love that he's so great with Logan. And the fact that my son likes and looks up to him. It warms my heart seeing them together.

I pull my phone out. And send a message.

Me: Thanks again for the rose. Both for me, and the one you gave Logan for Delany.

I try not to keep looking at my phone for a response. He's chaperoning. He needs to keep his eyes trained on the kids, not on his messages. My brain knows this, but my heart still hopes I'll hear the chime of a new message coming in. It takes five minutes and a million glances at my phone, but I see the dots on the screen.

Mason: Can't wait for you to thank me properly.

Me: With a kiss?

Mason: At a minimum.

I love how flirty he his. I love how Mason makes me feel. I love this silly giddy feeling I get when we talk or when we're together. I love . . . I stop right there. I don't allow myself to finish that thought.

I drop my phone on the counter as if touching it might prove fatal. What the hell is wrong with me? Mason is about here and now, about moving on and fulfilling needs and desires. He isn't about happily ever after. How I feel for him, it's not matching up to any of this.

I love him?

I can't. I don't. I won't allow myself to love him. I love my husband. Still. Always. Enjoying Mason's company is okay. Fantasizing about him through the day, who could blame me? Having the hottest sex of my life with him, that's an experience everyone isn't lucky enough to have. But love? It doesn't fit. Not for me. Not for him. Not at all.

*

"Hey mom, a bunch of kids are going to Burger Buster. Would you mind dropping us off?"

My eyes trail to Mason's car. It's still in the parking lot. He's still nowhere to be seen. Which is for the best. For some reason, unbeknownst to me, seeing his car leaves me with an empty feeling. Like something's missing, which is absolutely ridiculous since the car I'm driving belongs to him.

"Mom? Can we go?"

"What? I'm sorry." I glance at my son and his date through the rear view mirror. "Where did you want to go?"

"Burger Buster. Everyone's going to be there."

"We have to check with Delany's mother."

"I already did," she answers, with a sweet smile. "My mom said she's okay with it as long as you are. And she'll pick us up and drive us home so we don't have to bother you anymore."

"It's no bother, sweetheart. I'm happy to do it."

I drop the kids off and head back to my house. When I get back, I notice the time. It's about half an hour since the dance ended. I shouldn't expect to hear from Mason. I shouldn't expect anything from him, but the way he's been acting, it's hard not to. Didn't he say he wanted to see me tonight? Now that we both have free time, where the hell is he?

My phone chimes, and my heart leaps. I swallow hard, recognizing all the signs of an impending disaster.

Logan: Told you everyone was going to be here. Even Mr. Archer and Ms. Ferraro are here.

Along with the message is a picture of Mason and a beautiful young woman sitting at a booth. A rose lays on the table. They're looking at each other. Engaged in deep conversation, or staring into each other's eyes. I'm not sure which. It's a candid shot. He must not have seen Logan, or I doubt my son would've been able to snap this picture. For a variety of reasons.

Ms. Ferraro is young. Really young from what I remember. A first year teacher. She's beautiful, with long dark hair and chestnut eyes to match. I can't see her features well in the picture, but I see enough for it to hurt.

Mason is out with another woman. A young. Unattached. Beautiful woman. The type of woman he should be with. The type of woman he can build a future with. She'd be a fool not to be interested. Lord knows he's a great catch. And he deserves to be happy.

I don't respond to Logan's text. There's nothing to say.

Chapter 15

I change into an old pair of sweatpants, a worn, comfortable pajama shirt and sweep my hair up in a ponytail. I want to wallow in self-pity and be comfortable doing it. I fill a bowl with three large scoops of ice cream. I can't remember the last time I drowned my sorrow in comfort food.

When Keith died, I stopped eating. I lost twenty pounds in the first two months. It wasn't even the good kind of weight loss where you look fit and healthy. I looked sick. Drawn. Emaciated.

I kept ten pounds off, but my color returned and I'm happy with how I look. I don't know if I'll be able to say that after I finish off this bowl of ice-cream.

The ringing doorbell mid-spoon takes me by surprise. It can't be Logan, it's too soon, and he didn't text to tell me they're on their way back. I look through the peephole to see who it is.

Shit. It's Mason. I slide my back down the front door until I'm sitting on the floor. What the hell is he doing here? Probably came to tell me we can't see each other anymore because he has a new girlfriend.

Great and he gets to tell me while I look like a ragged old hag. I wish I didn't change out of my clothes. At least then I'd have a thread of dignity while he puts my heart through the ringer. I could just ignore him and pretend I'm not home. It's not like I expected him. Or like he bothered to call or send me a message.

My phone rings. I don't have to look. It's him. Sure, now he calls. It's not like I wasn't expecting this to happen at some point. I just wasn't expecting it to happen tonight. Time to put on my big girl panties and woman up. I stand, take a deep breath while I gather myself together and open the door.

Face to face with the man who is about to smash my heart into tiny pieces, I do my best to play it cool. I struggle to keep my emotions buried under the same mask I wore after my husband died.

Mason stares me up and down, with an amused look on his face.

"May I come in?"

I nod and step out of the way, opening the door for him to pass. He leans in and gives me a quick kiss on the lips. I don't reciprocate.

"New look?" He teases, but I'm not in the mood for laughs or games.

I shrug and turn away from him. "Just say what you came here to say."

"Amber." He grabs my arm and turns me around to face him. That wiped the smile off his face. His brows furrow and his blue eyes cloud with worry. "What's wrong?"

"Nothing," I pull out of his grasp.

"What the hell?" His tone is serious. "Tell me what's wrong?"

"Nothing," I say with as much defiance as I can muster up. "Nothing at all."

"Bullshit. Are you upset because Logan's out with a girl?"

I can't contain my frustration any more. I shake my head and look away, because looking at him weakens my resolve. And right now I need strength. Might as well get straight to the heart of the matter.

"No. I'm upset because *you* were out with a girl. Woman. Whatever. The point is, I just wish you would've been honest and told me."

Mason looks confused. "Do you mean Christina? We're just friends. We were both at the dance and she was feeling bummed because her boyfriend broke up with her last weekend."

"Look, I get why you'd want to be with her. She's young and gorgeous—"

"Yes. But not as gorgeous as you."

"Don't try to sugar coat it."

"Fine." His arms slip around my waist. "I won't sugar coat it. There's nothing going on with Christina because she's not you."

My body tenses, my hands grasp his forearms as I tell myself to push him away. As much as I want to, I can't bring myself to do it.

"Exactly." My voice cracks. "You can have something real with her. Something long term."

"That's not what I'm looking for."

"Maybe it should be."

"I can't believe Logan called to tell you I was out with another woman. Do you think he knows?"

"No. I think he was excited to see everyone, even you at Burger Buster. He sent me a picture." I break his hold on me and get my phone to pull up the heart wrenching image. Mason takes it from my hand and looks at the picture.

"I'm sorry, Amber. I had no idea he took this. I didn't know Logan wasn't coming home or else I would've been here sooner. The only reason I didn't come straight from the dance is because I thought it would be weird if I rushed over when I have no good reason to be here other than I want to spend time with you."

"You don't have to explain your actions."

"I do. Because as soon as I saw him at the diner, I wrapped things up with Christina. And I know how I'd feel if I saw a picture of you and another man like that. I'd have to go find you and kick his ass."

"It's fine, Mason." I lie, looking away to mask to the hurt.

"It's not fine. You're upset, and you have every right to be." He lets out a long breath. "I think we should come clean with Logan."

"No." I don't take a second to think about it.

"If we tell him, then I can be here with you, any time I want. We won't have to look for excuses and sneak around. And it will avoid misunderstandings like tonight."

"I said no!" I want him to drop the subject.

"Why the hell not?"

"Because he was close to his father. He idolized him."

"I understand, but Keith's not coming back, Amber."

"I know that!" My eyes sting and my voice betrays my weakness as I fight to hold the tears back.

"Maybe it's time Logan realizes it too."

"He does. Bedsides, how do you think he'll feel about his mother messing around with his coach?"

"Messing around?" There's a harshness to his voice I'm not used to. His angry eyes narrow. He's almost yelling at me. "Is that what we're doing?"

"Isn't it?" I snap. "It's not like there can be anything serious between us."

"Does this feel like we're just messing around? Because it doesn't to me. Not once since we started seeing each other did I think we are just messing around." He reaches a hand behind my head and grasps a handful of hair, forcing me to look at him. "Why can't there be anything serious between us?"

"You just said yourself you're not looking for long term."

"That's *not* what I said."

"Yes it is. Besides, look at you!" I try to pull away, break free from his touch, but he won't let me. "What are you twenty-three?"

"Twenty-seven. And I don't understand why you always go back to my age. What the hell does it have to do with anything?"

I close my eyes and take a breath. I need to slow down my racing heart and stop my hands, my entire body, from shaking.

"What kind of relationship could we have?" I ask, deflated. "I'm forty-three. That's sixteen years older than you. Hell, I could be your mother!"

Mason's strong, solid hands cup my face as he inches closer. "Amber, the only one that gives a fuck about the age difference is you."

I shake my head. "I'm not the only one. I won't be if people find out. And you *should* give a fuck."

"Why?"

"Because I have nothing to offer you. I'm at a different place in my life. I'm a widow with a teenage son. I'm done having kids."

"So?"

"Mason, you should be with someone that has more in common with you. Someone closer to your age."

His thumbs brush across my cheeks. "Just because a woman might be younger, it doesn't mean we have more in common. I understand you. I relate to you in a way I don't with twenty something year old women. Women," he scoffs. "They're girls. Insecure head cases full of drama and concerned with what I can do for them. The somewhat mature ones want to have kids like yesterday, or they're super-focused on their career and don't want kids."

"There's nothing wrong with working on your career. I'm focused on getting mine off the ground."

"You're different. I want to be with someone who has time for me. Someone I can talk to about my day who wants to share their day with me, not just yes me through dinner while she reads email off her phone. You don't do that. Even when you have a manuscript to get through. Younger women don't get how fleeting life can be. They don't understand what's really important, or how to make the most of each and every day. You do."

"Maybe you just haven't found the right girl yet."

"Maybe I have and she's an older woman."

"Don't say that."

"Why not? I feel more for you than I have for anyone in years. I wake up each day looking for an excuse to come over here so I can see you. Amber, I love you."

Silence hangs heavy between us.

Did he just say he loves me?

I must not have heard right. My heart pounds so fast and hard, you'd think I snorted a pound of coke. He messes with my head in that way, too. Makes me dizzy and out of control. Like I'm on a constant high when we're together.

Maybe I imagined those words. Or hallucinated. Drugs make you do that, don't they?

He's quiet. Worry shines through his eyes. He looks nervous. Scared even. He waits in silence, and I haven't said anything. Oh shit. *He did say it.* His words sink in. *I love you.*

I thought it was a one way road. I thought maybe I was an older woman fantasy he wanted to tick off his bucket list. Maybe I'd go so far as to say we are friends with benefits. I had no idea as I fought to stop myself from tumbling, he fell along with me. Side by side we journeyed together until we landed somewhere safe and scary.

In each other's heart.

I don't know who moves first; but I'm in Mason's arms, lips searching and kissing along his neck, across my jaw line, until they land on each other. I grasp his shirt pulling him closer. He crushes me against his chest holding me so tight I can barely breathe. His mouth crashes down on mine, teeth graze over my bottom lip. His tongue works its way into my mouth. Desperate. Passionate.

I pull Mason closer. It's not close enough. I need to feel him inside me. As if he knows what's on my mind, knows what I'm looking for, Mason presses his hips into mine.

"I love you," he whispers, in between the flurry of kisses he peppers down my neck. "I love you and I don't want to hear any more age bullshit. Understand?"

"Yes," I answer breathless, tilting my head back and enjoying the bombardment of my senses. "Oh, God, Mason," I moan. "I love you too!"

I didn't think it was possible. I thought my days of love and passion were behind me, but somehow he pushed and forced his way into my heart. I love him, and that's why thinking of him with another woman hurts so much because I found something I never expected. Love.

He reaches under my shirt and splays his hand flat on my stomach. His warm skin scorches as he slides his hand up to just beneath the band of my bra. I arch my back, wanting to feel his touch against my bare breast. Instead, he changes direction and inches his hand downward.

Without hesitation, his fingers slip under the elastic waistband of my sweatpants. I pull his shirt out of his pants, reach under it and run my hands along the solid muscles of his stomach and chest. I close my eyes and moan as his hand slips between my thighs and cups my mound. He rubs his hand back and forth over my panties, while I stroke the bulge straining against his pants.

"Hot and wet. Just the way I like you." He uses his tongue to caress the spot between my neck and my shoulder bringing tiny bumps to the surface of my skin.

I fumble with his belt buckle and the button of his pants. I need to get my hands under control.

"I'm always hot and wet for you." I let his pants fall and reach for his rock hard erection.

I take my time, pulling Mason's boxers down his legs as slow as I can, touching his skin as much as possible. Once they're around his ankles along with his pants, the Adonis in front of me kicks them off to the side.

I stand back to my full height and wrap my hand around his velvety shaft. I stroke up and down while using my free hand to unbutton his shirt.

"Tease." Mason grabs a hand full of hair and tugs gently. "It's been too long since I've been inside you. I don't know how much longer I can wait."

I take his hand, and lead Mason to the couch. When I have him where I want him, I push his chest, push him down to a sitting position. Mason looks up at me, his eyes filled with lust, and something else. Something I can't put my finger on.

He pulls me close, and kisses my lower abdomen while getting rid of my pants and underwear. His lips and tongue caress my hip, and move across to the top of my thigh. His mouth is warm and sends shivers up my spine. I want to feel his mouth, his tongue between my legs, but right now, I need more.

I push him back again taking charge and straddle his lap. I reach down with one hand and guide him inside of me. I keep my eyes locked on his as I slide down his length. Holding on to his shoulders, digging my fingers into his flesh, I move up and down, feeling him deep inside my body and my heart.

Mason lifts my shirt over my head and pulls down each bra cup so that my breasts bounce in front of him. After taking his time to fondle and suck on each one, his hands move to my hips. Faster and faster he guides me up and down.

His heavy lidded eyes make him look as if he's in a trance. Whatever spell he's under affects me as well. His breathing changes, and I know he's close. I am too. Mason grunts as he lifts me to the point where he's almost out of me and slams me back down while thrusting his hips upward.

I pulse and clench around him, hugging him tight. I whimper his name through labored breath, with no control of my body, or the quakes running through it.

"You better hurry and finish, babe. Because I'm so close!" He says, through gritted teeth.

With a loud cry, Mason's body picks up where mine finishes. His body tenses as his face contorts and loud grunts leave his mouth and swim to my ears. His hot seed drips out of me as I lean forward and gently bite his bottom lip.

Hot with sweat in my creases I rest my forehead against his. Our eyes lock on one another. Even though we don't speak, we communicate volumes in these moments. He smooths my hair and kisses my lips sweetly. We stay like this, staring at each other, breathing each other in, until my phone chimes.

"Fuck. That's Logan. We need to get dressed." I jump off Mason and start fixing my clothes.

I'm stopped by his hand on my elbow. "I love you, Amber, and nothing is going to change that. But I still think we should tell Logan. I don't like lying to him."

"I'll think about it, but now's not the time. You need to get out of here." I rush to gather Mason's pants and boxers.

"I'm not leaving."

I look into his eyes hoping he's joking. Hoping he wants a reaction from me. He doesn't.

"This isn't the time for games."

"I'm not playing games. I want to hear how things went with Delany."

"Mason!" I plead exacerbated.

"Amber, we got this. I promise." Mason kisses me one last time before disappearing into the bathroom.

God. I hope so, I whisper to myself as I watch him walk away.

Chapter 16

Love changes everything.

The blue of the sky looks deeper, more vibrant. Blooming flowers scent the air around us. The beautiful spring temperatures warm into hot days promising summer is near.

We're all in a good place. Logan spends time with Delany, both in and out of school. The band he's been working to put together over the last year is in place. He's happy. Productive. This allows me to be a little selfish and carve out some time for me. Which really means time with Mason.

He still eats dinner with us on Saturday nights. We "invite" him to join us when he comes to work with Logan earlier in the afternoon. We've taken to having longer meals. To help my cause, I serve more courses than usual when he eats with us, including soup, salad and dessert. Dinner takes so long, Logan gets bored half way through and leaves us alone.

I make excuses to get out of the house on weeknights. Getting coffee while I work, going to the grocery store. Meeting up with a friend. Logan never questions me. He takes me at my word, and it makes the situation a lot easier for me to deal with.

Sometimes I tell my son that I "ran into" Mr. Archer at the coffee shop, or the grocery store to explain why I was gone so long. Of course Logan isn't with me and doesn't realize I went shopping earlier in the day and hid a few bags in the trunk of my car. He has no idea these are excuses I make for my excursions when I sneak over to Mason's place.

But the emerging end of the school year threatens to end my free time. Before needing to make a firm decision about coming clean to Logan, I'd like a few days without Logan in the picture to thoroughly explore my relationship with Mason.

"Hey, Mom. Do you think Aunt Maggie will be upset if I want to come home early?" Logan asks shoving a sweatshirt into his duffle bag.

"No. But it's only for a few days. I know she misses you. And so do your cousins. Even though Dad isn't with us anymore, they are still family."

"I know." Logan looks down at the floor, and I wonder what's really going on. "But being with them makes me miss Dad."

"I know you miss him," I wrap my arm around my son's shoulder. And pull him close. I know he must be hurting bad because he isn't trying to shrug me off of him. "I miss him too. Like crazy."

"Does it get easier?"

I nod, and for once, I'm not lying. "It does. In the moments when you can laugh, or get lost in something you're passionate about, like when you're with Delany, or play guitar. In those moments, you sort of forget the pain. And it's okay to let it go."

"But then," his eyes fill with tears. "But then won't I forget him?" His voice cracks. "I don't want to forget Dad. Ever."

I understand Logan's fear. Now that Mason is in my life, I wonder the same thing. The deeper Mason invades my heart, the more I worry that I might forget the sound of Keith's voice, or the shine of his eyes when he spoke about Logan's latest accomplishment. But as of right now, they're still there.

"No sweetheart." I pull him into my arms. "You'll never forget Dad. He's a part of you. If you listen carefully enough, when you're quiet and alone, you'll hear him whisper straight into your heart."

Logan shakes his head.

"If you want to come home early, if it's too much for you, all you ever have to do is call me. No matter how old you get or how far from home you are, I'll come for you."

Logan sniffs, and to my surprise, throws his arms around me and leans in for a hug, I kiss the side of his head, content with where we are right now.

"And if you ask, I bet aunt Maggie will be happy to show you some funny pics of dad the first time he came home drunk from a party. He was passed out and she put make-up on him and took pictures. Then she had some blown up and replaced the family photos in the frames around the house with them."

"Really?"

"Uh huh. He never went home drunk again."

Logan laughs. I think spending this weekend with Keith's sister will be good for him.

"She has a lot of funny stories about your father growing up. Ask her about them, I'm sure it will feel good for her to tell them."

"Okay, Mom." Sadness fills my son's eyes again.

"You were happy like five seconds ago. Honey, what's wrong?"

"Will you be okay with me gone? I mean, won't you be lonely?"

I give him a reassuring smile. "I'll be fine. And I promise, I won't be sitting at home miserable. I think it's time to go out a little. What do you think about that?"

Logan nods. "I think it's a great idea."

*

"Morning sexy."

Fresh from the shower, Mason comes behind me with damp skin and cages me against the small center island. I close my eyes and moan as his lips brush along my shoulder. He steps in closer, pressing his towel covered lower half against me.

"You smell good." I smile enjoying the closeness.

"So do you." He takes my earlobe in his mouth and caresses it.

"I smell like sex." I sip my coffee pretending he has no effect on me while I work to ignore the familiar tingling of my body when he's near.

"Sex mixed with me. Best smell ever."

I turn in his arms to face him and brush my fingers through his damp hair.

"Why do you look so sad?" Mason cups my face with his big, strong hands. His eyes are heavy with emotion. He looks so young and so breathtakingly handsome.

"I'm not sad," I lie. "I'm just not a morning person."

He presses his lips against mine "That's because you don't wake up with me. You've seemed to like the mornings just fine while you've been here."

He's right. I've spent the last three nights with him. Three incredible nights of long baths with scented candles, sensual massages and lots and lots of sex. Sex when we wake up. Sex when we go to sleep. Sex anytime in between.

"My mother texted me the recipe for her cheesecake brownies."

"Those were amazing!"

"It's her way of saying she approves of you."

"I don't know about that." My eyes fall.

He lifts my chin with his crooked index finger. "She wouldn't have sent it if she didn't like you. She's kind of weird like that. She only shares her recipes with people she finds worthy."

I offer a resigned smile. "I don't know Mason, I think she's being polite."

He presses his lips against mine for a chaste kiss. "Don't get me wrong," he says between kisses on my neck that have me melting in his arms. "She likes you. Not as much as I do, but she likes you."

I think back to the previous night and dinner with his parents. I didn't expect the warm reception his parents greeted us with.

"My parents like you," he says, his hands slipping under the oversized t-shirt that keeps most of my intimate parts covered. "And my best friend loves you. As far as I'm concerned all the boxes are checked."

"It didn't take much to win Corey over."

"I know you're pretty special," Corey teases over our diner of Chinese take-out. "Nothing freaks Mason out the way you did."

"I wasn't freaked out and it wasn't anything Amber did."

"You threatened to kick my ass if I didn't get the Mustang and garage door opener over to her house within the hour."

"And it took you longer, which means I owe you a beating." Mason tosses a crumpled napkin at his friend.

"I needed time to find a locksmith available to come that night."

While Mason and his buddy go back and forth I head into the kitchen to replenish the empty beer bottles sitting on the coffee table.

"Let me help you." I close my eyes at the sound of Gina's voice. While Corey is friendly enough, she hasn't said much and when she does speak or throw a smile my way I feel like a dig comes along with it.

"So," Gina starts as I reach into the fridge and pull a couple of bottles out. "How did you guys meet?"

I hand her two bottles and take her head on as I reach back in for more. "Mason volunteered at the old age home where I live and after he fed me my applesauce and put me to bed for the night—"

She interrupts with a hand on my arm before I finish. "I'm sorry. I don't mean to come across as a bitch. I just didn't expect—"

"For me to be so old?"

"I guess."

"It doesn't bother Mason or me," I lie. "So I don't see how it's any of your business."

Gina stands frozen, open mouthed for a moment. "I'm sorry," she says with a guilty look on her face. "I didn't mean to judge. I'm just surprised."

"It's fine," I assure her. "It's my issue." I offer a forced smile. "We're bound to get funny looks and lots of questions so I better get used to it."

"Yeah, but Mason's happy. He doesn't date a lot. At least no one he introduces us to. He's really a sweet guy. Don't hurt him. He's been through a lot and he's like family to Corey and me."

"The last thing I want is to hurt Mason."

"Then we're all good," she says with a smile, turning and heading back into the living room.

Bringing me back to the moment, Mason slides his hands over my breasts. "Your tits are amazing," he says taking hold and squeezing them. "You shouldn't hide them." He pulls the oversized t-shirt he lent me up over my head.

He looks me over approvingly as I stand before him fully exposed. As if to even the score, he loosens the towel around his hips and lets it fall to the ground. I'm sure my eyes mirror the same greedy longings in his.

I love his body. With or without clothes.

"Bet I can cheer you up and make you forget whatever has you looking so sad." Mason says.

"Oh yeah? You think you know me that well?"

He nods with a crooked smile playing on his lips. "Um hum. Now I do."

Before I know it, Mason turns me around so that my back is to him once again. He plays with the peak of my nipples as he trails a path of kisses down my spine. His lips and tongue caress my skin covering me in tiny bumps making me shiver. His hands lag behind rubbing up and down my back, sending bolts of electricity through me.

His mouth finds my hip and he sucks and nips at the tender skin while continuing to explore my lower body with his hands. My pulse races as his fingers find my nerve center and he stands to his full height behind me.

He presses his lower half against mine, long, hard and precariously close to my entrance as his hands and mouth work on bringing me to the edge of another orgasm.

"It could be like this, Amber," he whispers. "I can make you cum over coffee every morning and then again at night."

His warm breath against my skin makes me shiver as my body tenses, searching for release.

It doesn't take long before I'm screaming out his name. My body trembles and shakes. My legs feel like jelly. I don't think I can stand. Before I can turn around and face him, Mason pushes my back down.

"My turn, baby."

I lean over the counter and hold onto the side opposite me as he's quick to press his shaft into me. Maybe because I feel so physically weak, or maybe I'm just more relaxed because of the countless number of orgasms over the last few days, but another one swells and grows inside me, almost from the moment he enters me.

It takes almost no time for me to cum again. This spurs Mason on to thrust harder. Faster. He leans over so that his chest is pressed against my back, his hands hold onto my breasts, and his head rests on mine.

There's something different about this time. The sex is amazing. The best it's ever been, but there's something more. I feel connected to Mason on every level. Physically. Mentally. Spiritually. I feel more connected to him than I've felt to anyone. Including Keith.

This realization unsettles me.

After cumming, Mason pulls out of me. He turns me around, holds my face and kisses me, long and deep. I feel the strength of his emotions in his kiss. I wonder if he could feel how guilty, how conflicted I am. I break away and lean my head against his warm chest, listening to his heartbeat. I love the sound and can't get enough of it.

I want to be with Mason, I have no doubt about that anymore. But am I a terrible person for it? Have I waited long enough to start dating? Does this mean I wasn't as happy with Keith as I thought I was?

Mason lifts my chin with his pointer finger forcing me to look up into the most beautiful blue eyes I've ever seen. "Do I wan't to know what's running through that beautiful head of yours?"

It's not hard to find a genuine smile when I look at him. When I'm with him, happiness infects me.

"Just that I love you. These past few days have been some of the best I've had in a really long time. Maybe ever."

"We'll have a lot more. I promise."

"Stealing time away together won't be so easy."

"It can be." He strokes my hair. "Let's be honest. Once Logan knows, we won't have to hide and sneak around. We can just be us, without any pretense."

I think about telling my son I'm in love with Mason. I don't know how he'll react. I do know that they have a pretty good relationship, so maybe Logan will be happy that we're together. Maybe Logan will embrace it faster and easier than I did.

"Okay." I can't believe I'm agreeing to this. "We'll tell him. But not as soon as he gets home. We'll tell him when you come over for dinner Saturday night."

"Are you sure? I think it's the right thing to do, but I don't want to pressure you."

I nod. "Positive."

Chapter 17

I take a batch of Logan's favorite cookies out of the oven while he sits at the kitchen table telling me all about his visit with his aunt and cousins.

"I'm so glad you didn't let me back out of going."

"I knew you'd enjoy yourself."

"Thanks Mom."

Logan gives me a hug, doing his best to touch me as little as possible while doing it. I can't wait till we get past these awkward teenage years and he's more confident in who he is again. We stay up late talking and laughing. To my surprise, Logan asks to go through our digital pictures together so that I can tell him the stories behind the photos when he was a baby.

Sitting together and laughing I enjoy reflecting on the memories. I haven't looked at these pictures in a while because the memories bring the sharp pain of missing Keith to the surface. This is the first time in two years I'm excited to replay those moments in my mind.

"I never saw Dad so beside himself as he was with you this day." I increase the size of the picture of Logan as a toddler with a very dark background. "You took all the pots and pans out of the cabinet and crawled in, all the way in the back, and it was so deep, it was hard to get you out."

A chill kisses my skin and it's covered with goose bumps. I'm not cold on the inside though. I feel a warmth in my chest. A healing warmth, and I feel like it's a hug from Keith. I close my eyes, and I swear I can almost smell his cologne.

I know it's crazy. I'm grasping for straws when there's nothing but air. At first I wonder if this is more guilt over my feelings for Mason. I know it's not, because thinking of the new man in my life doesn't hurt at all. Instead of tearing up and falling apart, I'm at peace. Soothed.

"Hey, Mom," Logan comes out of his room while I rinse the dishes off and place them in the dishwasher. "Delany invited me over after school tomorrow. Is it okay if I go hangout with her?

"Of course."

"Awesome."

I grab my phone when I get into bed. No messages. Then again, I'm not surprised. Mason said he didn't want to impede on my time with Logan. I want him to know he's on my mind.

Me: I miss you.

Mason: Can't wait for you to show me how much next time I see you.

Me: How about you direct me and I'll put on a show?

Mason: I can't wait.

Me: Sweet dreams.

Mason: Only if they're of you.

I lie back in bed, relaxed, happy, ready for tomorrow. No matter what it brings. My life is finally back on track.

*

After dropping Logan off at Delany's house, I head over to Mason's. The second I walk through the door, we're pawing at each other as if we haven't seen each other in months rather than twenty hours. Mason wastes no time getting me out of my clothes and tossing his to the ground.

Still in the hallway, he pulls me to the floor and climbs on top of me. Once Mason enters me, his fingers dig into my flesh. He takes me with need. Although his movements are hurried, I enjoy it as much as when we have time to linger in bed.

Once we satisfy our physical need to be together, we spend the next hour and a half snuggled together on the couch. Talking. Joking around. My phone alarm chimes and I know it's time to pick Logan up.

"This is going to be the longest week of my life," Mason says, walking me to the door.

"I know. I'll need to come up with a shit-ton of excuses to sneak over here." I step out of the front door.

"Wait!" Mason reaches for my hand and pulls me back. "One more kiss to hold me over."

"I'm a sucker for those blue eyes of yours."

"I'm a sucker for you."

Mason's lips brush against mine, soft and gentle. If this kiss is meant to hold him over, I want it to rile him up, make him hard and horny so that he thinks of me every minute until we see each other again. I press my chest against his, wind my fingers in his hair and swipe my tongue across his lips.

"Mmm." Mason's fingers thread through my hair. He holds me close and deepens the kiss.

"I really have to go."

"I know. It's just so hard watching you leave."

"Just a few more days before we tell Logan. Then it won't be so hard."

"I know. Now get going before I pull you back in the house and have my way with you."

*

I notice the sign as soon as I pull up to Delany's house. It's pretty hard to miss. For Sale stands out in big, bold letters. I have a bad feeling in the pit of my stomach. She's moving. I hope it's not far. Logan's going to be crushed.

I don't blame her mother. It's hard to live as if your husband is going to walk through the door one day when you know he's not. That he never will. I thought about moving after Keith died, because it hurt so much to be in our house without him. I couldn't bring myself to pack up his things and leave the home we shared. Because it was ours. It will always be ours. If I move, where ever I go it will just be mine, and Keith's presence in my life will be erased.

I know that's not really the case. I carry my husband around in my heart. In the memories and the traditions we started that I keep up. It's in my head that I can't rationalize moving. Even though being in our house hurts, brings flashbacks of things we said or did in virtually every spot, I have a hard time moving on.

At least I did, before Mason.

It's different being married to a cop. Every time he walks out the door, you're left wondering if he'll be home that night. If you'll ever see him again. And if you do, will it be dead or alive? It's a risk they take to serve and protect. A risk your whole family takes on.

Logan gets in the car and slams the door. He slouches down in his seat. *Oh yeah, this is hitting him hard.* Maybe this isn't the right time to tell Logan about Mason and me. He has enough on his plate.

*

"Delany's moving," I tell Mason the next night when we "accidentally" run into each other at Starbucks.

"So?"

"Maybe we should wait to tell Logan?"

With his hands folded in front of his mouth, Mason leans across the table. "Why not just rip the Band-Aid off all at once?"

"Because I'm worried about him."

"You said he was happy and had a great time with your sister-in-law last weekend."

"He did. He was. But now he's upset and depressed."

"I promise, it's going to be okay." Mason reaches out to touch me. I scan the shop to make sure no one is looking. Seeing my reaction, Mason retracts his hand. He leans back in his chair and lets out a long breath. "Whatever. We'll play it your way."

"You're upset."

"I'm frustrated." There's something hard in his eyes. Like he covered them with an invisible wall. "I thought we were in a good place."

"We were. I mean we are." I whisper shout. "This has nothing to do with you and me. This is just about doing what's right for my son."

"You're wrong." He gets to his feet and pushes his chair in. "It has everything to do with you and me."

With his coffee in hand, I watch Mason walk out. I had no idea how hard it would be to watch him turn his back on me and leave. Sure he does it when we're at my house, but it's never been like this. Never because he's upset with me.

I hurt him. That was never my intention. I'm only trying to do what's right. To be a good mother. It wrenches my heart that I can't run over to the man I love and ease his pain. I don't rush to leave. I sit at our table feeling like shit.

If we tell Logan it might hurt him and he's already going through so much. Or my son might be excited to have Mason around more. Someone he feels close too. Someone he confides in. If we don't tell, it definitely hurts Mason. And that's the last thing I want to do.

At home, I keep checking my phone for a text message. There are none. I shut my phone off and reboot it, just in case it's not working right. No such luck. By the time I'm ready to go to sleep, I break.

Me: I'm sorry. I love you so much, I don't want to hurt you. We'll tell him Saturday as planned.

It takes him longer than usual to respond. I close my eyes hoping sleep will find me so I can stop reliving that conversation. I want to forget the disappointment in his eyes.

Unfortunately I'm wide awake. Just when I've lost hope of him getting back to me, my phone chimes.

Mason: I'm acting like a douche aren't I? Sorry. I was looking forward to being with you out in the open. I can wait as long as you need me to.

Me: No. You're right. We should do this. Besides, it's better that he hears it from us. It was so hard not to kiss you tonight.

Mason: I wanted to do much more than kiss you. I wanted to touch you, too. Touch you in ways that would stir up the rumor mill ;-).

Mason is back to being lighthearted and fun. I feel better. Now I can sleep.

Chapter 18

This must be the longest week in the history of the world. Each day drags on, and Logan's mood only gets worse. I'm really nervous that coming clean about Mason and I will push him over the edge, but I won't back out of it. And I won't tell Mason about my reservations.

The closer it gets to Saturday the more nervous I am. Friday morning, I spend an hour doing yoga and meditating to relax. One more day. I can make it through one more day.

My phone rings. I check the caller ID. It's Logan's school. I answer the call hoping it's Mason.

"Mrs. Collins?"

"Yes."

"This is Mr. Butler from Roosevelt Middle School. I'm calling to let you know that Logan will be staying after school today to serve detention for smoking in the bathroom. Our policy is such that a parent must come in and sign the student out of detention before they are released. This way it is documented that you are aware of the infringement."

"Okay. Thank you."

I hang up shocked. My son was caught smoking? He knows better than to do that. Keith's father suffers from COPD and is on oxygen twenty-four hours a day. And school will be over in one week. He just needed to get through this last week without any drama. This doesn't make any sense.

Minutes later, a text comes in from Mason.

Mason: I'm coming over right after school. We need to talk.

Great. Those words are never good. Never a sign that something good happened, like he won the lottery or just got offered his dream job. No. It connotes a draining, emotional conversation. Like I need more shit thrown at me today.

*

"I'm waiting for an explanation." I snap at my son who hasn't said a word since I picked him up from detention at school. I'm so frustrated with him! Just when I thought we've made it to a good place, everything blows up in my face.

The worst part was having to get the call from Mr. Butler. Smug bastard. He sounded way too happy to tell me that my son was in detention.

"Smoking, Logan? What the hell is wrong with you? You know better than to fill your lungs with that shit. And what were you thinking doing it in school?"

"I wasn't smoking."

"Well then, do you want to explain why you had detention for smoking in the boys room?"

We're interrupted by the doorbell. Great. Mason. I don't know if I can deal with whatever is bothering him at the moment. My hands are beyond full with Logan.

"Don't answer," Logan orders.

"It's probably, Mr. Archer."

"Exactly. He can go fuck himself."

"Logan!" *What the hell has come over him?* "You owe me and Mason an apology," I say heading for the door.

"Don't call him that! And don't let him in!" Anger rolls off my son in large, overpowering waves. I'm afraid he's going to get swept up and pulled away in the ocean of emotion he's swimming in.

"What is your problem?" I ask as I open the door. There's no answer. I look over my shoulder to find Logan's no longer there. My son retreated to his room, or the bathroom, or somewhere else in the house. Too bad. We aren't done discussing what happened.

"This isn't a good time," I say to the stoic man standing in front of me.

Mason ignores me and gives me a quick peck on the lips. His eyes though, they never meet mine. They search the room behind me.

"Where is he?"

"Logan?" I don't know why I ask. He's the only one Mason could be referring to.

"I don't know, I think he snuck into his room when I answered the door."

"Call him out here. We need to talk. Now."

My spine stiffens. I don't like being given orders, let alone about my son. I don't lace into Mason just yet, because I have a feeling this is about Logan's detention and Mason has done a lot for Logan. Like me, he probably feels betrayed.

Mason's jaw is clenched, his normally playful eyes are dark and angry.

My blood runs cold.

"Logan!" Mason calls. "Get out here, or I'm coming in to get you."

"Fuck you!" My son replies.

"Logan!" I can't believe he just said that. I'm embarrassed, and I have no idea what's prompting his irrational behavior. "Logan! Get out here now and apologize!"

Logan joins us in the living room. His eyes are small and narrow, his face red. His laser like stare focuses on Mason.

"Leave!"

"No. I'm telling your mother."

"You're a fucking liar!"

With anger chiseled on his face, Mason advances on my son. My stomach nosedives to the ground and my heart squeals, agonizing over watching this confrontation between the two most important people in my life.

What the hell happened?

I don't think Mason would lay a finger on my son, but that's a risk I can't take. I can't wait to see how this plays out. I rush to stand between them.

"You better watch that mouth of yours," he warns.

"Or what?" Now it's Logan that's advancing. His shoulders are squared, as if he's challenging Mason. I can't imagine what's gotten into him or what he's thinking. "What are you going to do about it? You're not my father. You can't tell me what to do."

"I put my ass on the line for you today. It's not going to happened again."

"You gave me detention."

"For smoking. If I told the truth, you would've been expelled and the police would be here right now, searching every inch of your house. I'm not about to let this go. We're going to deal with this here and now. Understand?"

"Fuck you! I hate you!"

They're too close for comfort, only feet away from each other. I can feel the anger between them. It's raw and explosive, and I have no idea what to do. I turn sideways with one hand on Mason's chest, hoping this will be enough to keep him from moving forward. Still lost as to what brought this about, I focus my attention on my son.

"You're grounded. Give me your phone." I say, wondering why Logan's death stare is still focused on Mason. "Now!"

Logan clenches his jaw as he pulls his phone from his pocket and starts messing with it.

"I said give it to me now!" I step up and grab the phone out of his hands.

"Look!" Logan yells. "Look what he did!"

I don't. The last thing I want is to give Logan the satisfaction of looking or giving him the impression that I'm taking his side.

"Amber, you need to know the truth."

"You don't know anything you worthless piece of shit!" Logan's face is red, flushed. The veins in his neck bulge and rise to the surface. I've never seen him like this.

"I know what you were doing with that low life in the bathroom. I know what that money was for."

Money? What money? Logan was caught smoking, but is there more? Is that what this is all about?

"He's lying, Mom. Don't listen to him."

"Drugs?" I ask Mason.

He nods his head. "He tried to buy roofies."

Roofies?

The blood drains from my head. I'm dizzy. Blackness creeps in around me. It advances from both sides at once. Darkness threatens to swoop me away from this moment, to shut it all down until I can wake and find it's all a bad dream.

It feels like a giant mallet is stuck inside my head, working to make its way out. Nausea has me clenching my stomach as bile rises up my throat, into my mouth. I swallow hard and force it back down. My knees are weak. I don't think I can stand any longer, I'm about to drop, when strong arms wrap around me and lend me strength.

"Roofies?" I ask looking into the ocean of blue I learned to trust. The eyes that taught me to love again. The words are barely audible. Not more than a whisper. I shake my head as tears blur my vision.

Logan stares at me. Angry. Frightened. Shaking his head.

"Get your hands off my mother." He growls, his voice low and threatening.

"Logan, you need to stop." Mason snaps. "Let her breathe a minute before she passes out."

"What were you going to do with roofies?" I ask, unable to believe we're having this conversation. Drugs are bad, but I might understand if he wanted to chemically alter his mood and feelings, but roofies aren't for him, they're for him to use on someone else.

"I was going to plant them. On him!" Logan points at Mason. "To ruin him so he'd lose his job and go to jail."

My heart splinters and shatters with each passing second. *How did this happen?*

Slowly, with the safety and security of Mason's arms around me, I drop to the floor.

"You want to ruin me?" Mason asks, the anger that was there a moment ago is replaced by surprise. "What . . . Why?"

Tears stream out of Logan's angry eyes. His hands are balled up into tight fists. I can see a war raging inside him.

"I thought you were there for me. I thought I could trust you." He uses the back of his fists to clear the tears from his face. "But it was never about helping me. You used me to get to my mother." He stops and gulps in a long, deep breath. "You just wanted to fuck my mother and now everyone knows, and everyone's laughing at her. Calling her names."

Logan's hands fly up to his head. It looks like he's in pain. Like he's trying to stop it all by crushing his head between his hands.

"Logan, I *was* there for you. I still *am*. I want to help you. That's why I covered for you today, but this is serious. I can't do that again." Mason's tone is much softer than it's been since he got here.

"Liar!"

"I'm not lying, Logan. Look, you're a great kid, and this really was all about you in the beginning but somewhere along the way, I fell in love with your mother."

"You don't love her! If you loved her, you would've told me. She wouldn't be your dirty little secret."

And there it is. I fucked up. It's all on me.

"She's not. I'd never think of her like that."

I have to step in. I have to say something. Own up to the mistakes I made in all of this.

"Logan, honey." I fight the tears and the jumble of emotions overwhelming me at the moment. "Mason wanted to tell you. From the beginning. It was my decision not to. We were going to tell you tomorrow night."

"Why? Why wouldn't you want me to know?" He sounds like he did when he was a little boy and thought something was unfair.

"I didn't want to upset you."

"Upset me? You didn't want to upset me?" He shakes his head. "You're no better than him. I hate you both." Logan runs off to his room and slams the door behind him.

Mason drops to his knees and joins me on the floor. "I'm sorry, Amber."

He wraps me up in his warmth and strength, and kisses me on the head.

"He wanted me to see something." I press the home button on Logan's phone twice, and it brings me right into his Instagram account. Right to a picture of me kissing Mason outside his front door.

Next to it the person who posted it wrote "Bet that's why Logan made the team. He sucks." Followed by a stream of nasty hashtags. #Archersbitch #ArchersSlut #MotherFucker #SlutMom #CockSuckingMom. On and on they go.

I'm numb, and shutting down again. Locking up my heart. The way I did after Keith died. It's how I dealt with the pain. It's how I survived, because pain this deep, pain this sharp does nothing good. It just kills you slowly.

Mason smooths my hair and kisses the top of my head, before pulling it to rest against his chest. I take a moment to enjoy the feel of his arms. To feel and hear his heart beat against my face. To breathe him in.

I try to code it all into memory. His voice. His touch. His scent. I don't want to forget anything. I already forgot too much about my husband. At least these memories are fresh, so I can pull them from my heart when I need strength to make it through the day.

"Let's give him some time to cool down. In the meantime we can get him some help and then talk through this rationally. The three of us. Together."

I don't answer. I just stare at the screen. At the hashtags. At the comments. No wonder Logan went off the deep end. We betrayed him. I have to do what I should've done from the beginning. I have to say goodbye to Mason and refocus on my son. Four short years and he'll be off to college. Then I can have a life.

Maybe.

"Amber, you're too quiet. I need you to say something."

Why does he have to push this? Why is he rushing to say goodbye? I don't answer, hoping he'll drop it. Hoping I can hold him close for a few more minutes. Hoping we can find peace and comfort in each other's arms.

"Amber?"

"Mason, I'm sorry." My broken voice gives me away.

"No, Ambs. Don't. He's acting out. He'll get over it."

"How do you get over a picture of your mother and her twenty something year old boyfriend labeled cock sucking mother on the internet? How?"

Mason shakes his head and closes his eyes. "I'm telling you, we'll get him in therapy. We'll go with him and he'll come around. We'll teach him methods to cope—"

"He's about to start high school. The whole school, all his friends, everyone he knows is going to talk about this and look at him different. This isn't something he should have to learn to cope with. I'm sorry, but the only thing I can do, the right thing is for us to stop seeing each other."

"The right thing? For who? For you? For me? Don't we count? Don't we get a say?"

"We do. I'm giving you my say."

Mason gets to his feet, leaving me in a puddle on the floor.

"You didn't listen when I said we should tell him. Listen to me now. I love you. For the first time in years I see love and a family in my future. We're worth the risk, and I promise Logan's going to come out of this better. Stronger."

"Did you hear him, Mason?" I squeal. "He wanted to hurt you. Ruin you. And he didn't care how he did it," my voice drops. "If he got his hands on those drugs and got caught . . . He'd have no future."

"Glad you're not worried about what it would've done to me."

"Of course I am! If Logan did anything to hurt you," my voice cracks, and I refuse to let the tears flow. I'm too strong for tears. Too tough to cry. I rather choke it all down and fall apart when I'm alone. Like I used to. "If my son destroyed the man I love, it would shatter me. So I refuse to put either of you in that position any longer."

"You're not doing this for me. Not at all. You're doing this because Logan threw a tantrum. Yes, the shit he showed you is hurtful, but you're not teaching him to deal in the real world. You're sheltering him, and he doesn't know how to focus his anger into something positive. I could help with that. That's what you're taking away from him. That's what you're cheating him out of."

Is he implying that I'm not a good mother? I've been both mother and father to my son for the last two years. When he was younger I spent long nights awake with Logan, soothing him when he was sick. I cook and clean and cater to him. Chauffeur him all around town so he doesn't have to miss anything. I dedicated my life to my son and this is what I get? Told by some man that hasn't been here for more than a hot minute that I'm failing him? *Oh, fuck no.*

"You need to leave. Now."

"You don't mean this."

"Yes!" I snap. "Yes, I do!"

Mason stares at me like I'm a stranger for a long moment before he makes a move.

"Fine. You made your decision. Just know that this is your choice. You're ending it. You're sending me on my way."

"I understand."

"Good. Then understand if I walk out that door, I'm not coming back."

"Just go." I watch him walk away from me, devastated. Broken. A shell of what I was when he walked into my life.

Chapter 19

Two weeks pass and Logan still won't talk to me. He won't even look at me, which is the most gut-wrenching part of all. Not even in therapy, which he resents me for even more. I don't know how much more of this I can take.

I'm his mother. I felt him grow and live inside me. I dedicated my life to him. He's why I gave up my career. So I can stay home and give him the upbringing Keith and I didn't have because we each had both of our parents working.

And now my son wants nothing to do with me.

He won't eat anything I prepare. I cook dinner. Make him lunch. Put cereal in a bowl in the morning, and he doesn't touch any of it. I know he's eating though. I hear Logan rummage around the kitchen late at night when I'm in bed.

I give him more lea-way than I should, than I would if his father was here. But that is precisely the reason I'm so lenient. I carry around a great big ball of guilt that he doesn't have his father, as if I had something to do with it.

Keith's loss is just as trying, just as stressful, for me as it is for Logan, and that makes dealing with this situation on my own that much harder. I hold it all in. All the hurt. All the guilt. All the shit wearing me down hour by hour until I'm alone at night and I can cry and hate the world for doing me wrong.

Unlike when Keith died, I don't have anyone to turn to. No one to talk to. No shoulder to cry on. I never told my parents or my friends about Mason, so I can't let them know how broken hearted I am. They wouldn't believe me even if I tried.

It hits me. A great big ugly truth slaps me in the face like a cold, dead fish.

I was never Mason's dirty little secret like Logan accused. Never ever. Mason wanted to take me out. He introduced me to his parents and friends. Mason never treated me like a one night stand or someone he was just messing around with.

No, I wasn't ever *his* dirty little secret. *He* was mine. I never said it, never even thought it, but my actions spoke louder than words ever could.

No wonder I haven't heard from him. I didn't think it was possible to feel worse than I did a minute ago. But I do. This is by far the lowest point of my life. And for a change it's not the emptiness of losing Keith that has me unable to function. It's loosing Mason.

Time passes whether you want it to or not. You can lie in bed with your head under the covers and hide away from the world for days on end, but the clock keeps ticking. Nothing slows it down or stops it.

A month passed since I kicked Mason out of my life. An entire, long, lonely month with nothing to look forward to. I'm going stir crazy. I have a hard time with the silence in the house and on my phone. I'm not even comfortable in my own skin.

I look at my left hand. My wedding band still sits on my finger. I never bothered taking it off after Keith died. I couldn't bring myself to do it. I twist it around my finger and pull. It slips off easily. I hold it and admire the twinkling of the tiny diamond chips along the perimeter of the band.

The ring is endless. A symbol of infinite love. Just like my love for Keith and his love for me. I clasp it tight in my fist and hold it against my chest. I don't need to wear my wedding band to remember my husband. Just like I told Logan, Keith is in my heart. Forever. He's part of me, and nothing is going to change that. I place the ring in the jewelry box on my dresser.

I'm so far down in a never ending hole, I need to take some action to stop this free fall into nothingness. I shower, pull on a pair of yoga pants and a long shirt. I look like shit. My clothes don't fit right. I'm pale. My eyes have large dark bags underneath them. I'm not surprised. I haven't had a decent night's sleep in weeks.

Sleep isn't the only thing I haven't done. I can't hold down more than a few bites of food at a time and I haven't left the house. Except to take Logan to therapy and drop him off at the food pantry I have him volunteering at. I hope this will help him see the other side of what his little stunt could've done. It could've left Mason without a way to support himself. Without his reputation. Without anything.

I don't even leave to shop for groceries. I've been using the online delivery service the store offers. Who cares that it costs more? At least this way I don't have to find myself under the scrutiny of prying eyes. Eyes I'm sure have seen the viral image of me kissing Mason.

Bad enough I had to deal with the prying eyes and overly loud whispers at the middle school graduation. Thinking about it angers me. I need to snap out of this malaise. I'm hiding from the world. A prisoner to public opinion.

Why? Because I had a relationship with Mason? A kind, caring, sexy as hell man that happens to be younger than I am. So what? We're consenting adults. We did nothing wrong. Besides, what woman in her right mind wouldn't want to be with him if she had the opportunity?

I can handle the whispers and rumors. I could live with the scrutiny. It's Logan I worry about. And because of this, I've allowed my son to bully me into solitude. Last I checked he needs my permission to do things, not the other way around.

It's time for me to stop this madness. I miss Mason more than I thought possible. I didn't think anything could come close to how I felt in the early days of Keith's death, but this far surpasses it. At least then, I could lose myself in Logan. In taking care of him, making sure he was okay. Now I have nothing to help me through the day.

My stomach roils. I feel sick. I'm so upset, so worn down that even it wants nothing to do with me and works under protest. I want to crawl back into bed and close my eyes, but I don't. I force myself to put on make-up and get out of the house. Today is the first day of operation take back my life.

*

I type a message and delete it. I don't know what to say. I've already left an apology on Mason's voicemail. A few apologies. That was two weeks ago. He hasn't gotten back to me. It's probably time to move on and forget him, but I can't. He worked his way too deep in my heart.

Two weeks ago I forced myself to go shopping and buy something sexy. I planned to wear it and go to his house to not only say how sorry I am, but to show him. I went to a store that caters to the younger crowd and bought a short, tight dress.

I scheduled an appointment with a high class salon I never used before to have my hair and make-up done. I looked good. Really good. The make-up hid the bags and how sunken in my cheeks are. I hardly recognized myself.

At home I got dressed and took a last look in the mirror before I left. I turned from side to side admiring how good, how different, I looked. I didn't look like me at all. That was the problem. While my make-up never looked so good, the woman put it on so heavy, it looked and felt more like a mask than something to enhance my looks.

I chickened out of confronting Mason. I'd have no problem going to him like that if that was the norm, but not to apologize and try to win him back. He didn't fall in love with a slut version of me. He fell for who I am, not who I'm trying to be.

I've been forcing myself to leave the house, even though I'm bone tired most of the time. If I could sleep it wouldn't be so bad, but this half an hour at a time bullshit kills me. Sleep for half an hour stay awake for two hours. Every day is the same. Except lately I'm actually sleeping for two hours and awake for half an hour. I guess my body needs to make up for the sleep I lost. It's not like I'm twenty years old.

Today I'm going to brave the supermarket. Once I left the house I decided to go to one a few towns over where I don't know anyone. So far my strategy works. I don't see a familiar face. I can't hide forever. And the truth is, I don't want to. I'm too tired, mentally and physically. If someone has something to say, let them say it to my face.

On line to pay the cashier, my stomach makes a loud angry sound. I don't know the last time I ate. I can't stand to even look at food, let alone eat it. Another loud growl catches the attention of the cashier and the woman behind me. Both women smile sympathetically. I guess we all have our days.

After packing the groceries away in the car I walk to a pizzeria further down in the strip mall. Pizza's the healthiest fast food, and I don't feel like putting anything together at home. I walk in, place my order and look for a table to sit at.

My heart drops ten stories below the ground. Mason. A woman. Holding hands. Tears prick my eyes. I can try to be brave all I want, this time I won't succeed. He's not supposed to be here, out with another woman.

I shouldn't be surprised though. School's over. It's summer break, Mason has plenty of time to kill. No wonder he hasn't called or texted. He's moved on. So much for love. Guess his love doesn't run as deep as mine, because there's no way in hell I could even think about another man, let alone be out with one.

I want to change my order, and take it to go, but my stomach reminds me of why I'm here. It continues its campaign to humiliate and embarrass me. That's what I get for leaving it empty.

While I wait for my slice of pizza to be ready, I can't help myself. I gawk at them. She's a young blonde. Like his age or younger young. I shouldn't be surprised. But I am. I believed his lies, hook, line and sinker.

Once my dish is ready, I sit down at a table. I position myself so that I'm not facing them, not looking at them. But I can't help glancing over every few seconds. Wanting to eat even less now than I did when I got in here, I chew my food slowly.

"Ash, no!" His voice carries over to me.

Ash? Ashley. No wonder he looks so chummy with her. She's his first love. The one he wanted a future with. *The one.*

"Stop being so silly," she says with a smile in her voice. I hate her. "I'll be right back."

I watch her walk away looking for something, anything wrong with her. But I can't find anything. No ugly wart on her nose. No hunch in her back. Not one little imperfection.

Is it wrong to hate someone so vehemently just because they exist? I have no right, no reason to hate Ashly, but if the ceiling caved in right now and every piece of it fell on her head, I wouldn't be upset. In fact I'd cheer.

What has this man reduced me to?

He looks down into his soda, toying with the straw. He's much better at this game than me. I hate that while I'm here eating my heart out, he won't even look at me. Fine, I'll force him to look at me. I'll get in his face.

Before Ashley returns, I get out of my seat and approach Mason. His leg bounces under the table as our eyes meet. For the first time in six weeks, I get to fall into those oceans of blue. Only I can't bare looking at them because they're hard and cold. I focus on his lips. Lips that kissed every part of my body.

STOP!

I swallow hard and take a deep breath.

"I'm sorry."

"For?"

It's hard to find words. "I handled everything wrong. I should've listened to you. And I never should've let you leave."

He nods, but doesn't say anything. Why won't he say anything?

Ashley returns and slips into the booth across from Mason. I see questions in her eyes. I plan on being the one to answer them, but my stomach has other plans. My stomach spasms. Shit. I run from the table into the bathroom and heave.

I hate throwing up. Tears stream down my face even though I'm not crying, as a mixture of bile and pizza force their way out of my stomach. I didn't even eat that much. When I'm done in the bathroom, I spend time cleaning myself up: rinsing my face and swishing water around in my mouth.

I hope he's gone. The last thing I want to do now is face Mason.

Ashley waits for me outside the bathroom door. I was wrong. The last thing I want is to have to deal with Ashley.

"Would you like a ride home?" She asks, handing me my purse.

Is she being nice or does she want to rub my face in her relationship with Mason?

"No, thank you."

"I think we should talk."

"Please. I can't do this."

"Fine. Have it your way." She walks away, with a slight shake of her head. *Bitch*! Boy do I hate her.

Chapter 20

I fry meatballs at the stove when Logan walks through the front door unexpectedly.

"Logan," I call. "What are you doing home? You're supposed to be at the food pantry for another hour."

No answer.

I'm done with this. With his cold shoulder and one word answers. I'm so done. I've given him time and space, now it's time to shake him up and get in his face.

"If you don't get over here by the time I count to three, I'm coming in your room and taking a hammer to your guitar."

That does the trick. Counting always worked when he was younger and nothing seem to matter to him as much as his guitar. Especially now. His footsteps near.

"What?"

My mouth drops. His face has dried up blood, and his eye is a deep red, as if it's bruising. He's been fighting. I reach into the freezer, pull a bag of frozen peas from it, and hand it to him.

"What happened?"

"Nothing!" Logan holds the bag over his eye.

"Bullshit! Logan Michael Collins, I've had it with you. I am your mother, whether you like it or not, so enough of the cold shoulder bullshit, you're going to tell me what the hell is going on, or I'm calling the police and you could tell them."

"I'm fine. Okay? I just got into a scrape with the ass-wipe that threatened Delany. He came into the food pantry with his mother. He took pictures of me and said he was going to post them and tell everyone that we're so poor you were fucking Mr. Archer for money."

"No one would believe that."

"Everyone would believe that. They already do. Are you happy? Everyone in this shit town thinks you're a fucking prostitute. And I'm sick of hearing it. I wish you weren't my mother! Just leave me the fuck alone!"

I don't hear the end of my son's rant. It's as if someone shut my hearing off. And darkness creeps in all around me, from every angle. My head feels funny. Dizzy. I reach for Logan, but it's too late, I can't grab onto him, can't secure my feet on the ground.

I try to scream as my legs give way beneath me and I hit the ground.

I dream of Mason. It's the first good dream I've had since we broke up. The first time he speaks to me, and holds me, and assures me everything is going to be all right. I don't want to wake up. I want to stay here, where I'm happy.

"Mr. Archer. I'm so sorry! I didn't know who else to call, she just . . . she's been miserable and depressed, and I only make things worse." Logan rambles in a high pitched voice. "She fucking passed out and it's my fault. I'm such a shit. I was so mean, and I told her I didn't want her to be my mother."

"It's okay, Logan. She knows you didn't mean it."

"Yeah, but If she dies . . ."

"Whoa. Hold on. She's not going to die."

"You don't know that."

Logan's hysterical. I want to open my eyes and reassure him it's okay, that I forgive him, but I don't. Because I'm selfish. Mason is here, and I'm afraid the second I open my eyes, he's going to bolt out the door.

"Tell me what happened. Can you do that?"

Logan sniffles. "I left the food pantry early. I came home and she was cooking. And then she threatened to smash my guitar if I didn't come out of my room. She saw my face and freaked."

Someone strokes my hand before lifting it and rubbing their thumb back and forth. I can't mistake that touch. It's Mason. He's here and he's touching me.

"And then I said some really mean shit to her and she looked like she was reaching out for me, but I moved so she couldn't touch me. I didn't help her. I just let her fall," my son sobs. "I didn't know this was going to happen." His cries are muffled. Muted. I hope Mason's consoling him.

"Hey, whatever happened, it's not your fault. She loves you more than anything. Trust me, once she opens her eyes she's going to tell you just how much."

"No. I've been such a dick. To both of you. I can't believe you're even talking to me. Please, Mr. Archer, please make her better."

"Ah, Logan, all we can do is wait and see what the doctors have to say. As far as me being here, I told you I would, no matter what."

"That was before. I'm so sorry. Everything got so messed up and I had no control of anything. I didn't know what to do. So I fucked everything up. Why didn't you go to the police? Why don't you hate me?"

"Because I've been where you are. We do stupid things and lash out at the people that love us. Later we regret them. Don't get me wrong, I was seriously pissed at you. Still am. But I don't think you really want to ruin my life. Maybe you did in the moment, but not in a real way." I hear compassion and tenderness in Mason's voice.

"You came even though you're pissed? Why?" Logan sounds confused and broken.

"That's what you do when you love someone. You make sure you're there when they need you, no matter what."

"You really love her?"

A chair scrapes across the floor. "I do. Very much. I love the both of you. But I have a confession. I ran into her today, and I wasn't very nice. I wish I could do it over. I would've told her that I love her. That I'm mad as hell at her, but I'm losing my shit without her."

That's all I need to hear. My eyes flutter open. I turn toward the men I love. Logan notices first. He rushes over to the bedside and holds on to the guard rail.

"Mom! I'm so sorry I was such a dick. Just get better, and I'll never do anything like that again."

"Language," Mason warns.

"It's okay." My voice is lower than I expect. Weak. "I'm just glad you're here." I smile at my son.

Mason squeezes my hand and leans forward in the chair, closer to the bed.

" I'm glad you're here, too," I squeeze his hand back.

"How much of our conversation did you hear?" Mason asks with a smirk.

"Enough."

"Amber I—"

"It's okay. Can we talk about it later? I have a terrible headache."

He nods. "Is there anything I can get you?"

I look at the monitor I'm hooked up to, then up at the bag of clear liquid attached to an IV they placed in my other hand.

"I'd like something to drink. Some water or juice."

"Okay. I'll go check with your nurse to make sure it's oaky first."

Mason gets up and Logan takes his place.

He only sits for a minute when a very young male doctor enters the room and kicks Logan out.

"I love you, Mom," my son says before leaving.

"Are you feeling better?" The man asks with a smile.

"Much."

"You were dehydrated."

"I guess that's from throwing up so much. I don't even want to look at food."

"Well that's certainly not the answer. You need to eat, and make sure you drink a lot to counteract the morning sickness," he says moving his stethoscope around my belly. Otherwise you risk losing the baby."

"The what?" Mason and I say at the same time.

Once I heard morning sickness, I forgot about Mason and Logan and everyone else in the world besides the doctor. I didn't realize Mason came back in the room. I'm afraid to look at him. Afraid this is the straw that will drive him away for good.

The Doctor's eyes narrow on me. "You do know that you're pregnant don't you?"

I swallow hard, this can't be happening.

"No. There must be some mistake. I can't be pregnant."

"Why not?"

"Because I'm going through menopause."

"Did your doctor tell you that you couldn't get pregnant?"

"No, but I haven't had my period in half a year."

"You can go many months without ovulating, but then an egg drops at the right time, it's fertilized, and you're pregnant."

"Do we know how far along she is?" Mason asks.

"No. But since you didn't know, we could have someone come in and give you an ultrasound while your IV finishes. That should be able to give you an idea of when you're due."

The doctor leaves. Neither of us say anything. Mason hasn't moved.

"I didn't mean for this to happen." I say freaked out. "I had no idea. I thought I couldn't get pregnant."

He steps forward, puts the juice and straw down on the rolling table next to the bed. Mason takes my hand, he takes a long look into my eyes, and then a deep breath. Still no words leave his mouth.

"Mason? Are you oaky?"

He lets go of me and paces the small area next to my bed with both hands behind his neck.

"Mason, please say something. Anything."

He shakes his head. "Ashley told me you were throwing up in the bathroom. I didn't even consider that you might be pregnant."

Ashley. That's the one word I wish he didn't say.

"You're back with her."

Mason looks long and hard at me, his face, his eyes give nothing away. No confirmation. No denial.

"What do you want me to say, Amber? I mean you've made it perfectly clear you didn't want me. Every time something uncomfortable comes up, your instinct is to give up and run."

"I didn't run."

"No. You pushed me away."

"I wanted to protect my son."

He shakes his head. "That's exactly it. You made your decision and didn't care about what I thought. Is that how it's going to be with a baby? You're just going to dismiss whatever I think or feel because you know better? Because you've been through it before and I haven't?"

"I would never—"

"But you did."

"That's not what I did. Don't pervert what I did. Logan still has a hard time with losing his father. Keith and I didn't break up. We didn't disagree. He was killed by a drunk driver. I do the best I can with all of it." I pause for a beat and get back to the problem at hand. "Mason, this is different. I need to know, do you want this baby?"

"Does it matter what I want?"

"Of course it does. I love you. I didn't think it was possible to find love again, but I did. And I get that I blew it. I did everything wrong. Especially at the end. I understand that I hurt you. But that was never my intention."

"What do you want?"

"I don't know," I lie, afraid of his reaction.

I do know. I want Mason and this baby. This miracle baby that I didn't think could ever be conceived. I want us all to be a big happy family. But I let Mason go. Pushed him away and no matter how much he loves me, things are complicated now. I'm pregnant with a baby he doesn't want and it will no doubt have some bearing on his renewed relationship with Ashley.

"That's the problem." He crosses his arms over his chest. I've never seen his eyes so sad. His face is contorted with pain. "You don't know what you want. Including me."

"Mason please," I sit up and reach for his hand. He doesn't fight me. He allows me to take it, to hold on to him with both hands. "I don't know how or why this happened. Years ago, after Logan, Keith and I tried to have another baby, but I never conceived. He was tested. The problem was with me. I see this as some kind of miracle. I think we can both do with a bit of a miracle in our lives."

I'm wearing him down. I see his eyes softening.

"Great. You're pregnant. You can have this baby without me if you want."

"That's not what I want!" I can't take anymore. My resolve cracks. I think it's gone for good as tears streak down my face. "I want you, Mason. I love you, and I know this isn't the future you envisioned or planned for, but I want to do this with you as my partner. I want you by my side every step of the way."

He sits on the edge of the bed and strokes my hair, but I'm not done. I can't hold back, I need to get it all out and let the chips fall where they may.

"And I know that makes me selfish. I don't care. She doesn't deserve you. She cheated on you when you needed her the most. It's our time now. And I need you. Not because I'm pregnant. I need you because you taught me how to be happy again. How to make the most out of every day and find happiness when all I can see is sorrow." I cry and sound hysterical, but I don't care.

"I need you because you're my balance when I'm on the edge. You're my alternate point of view when I have blinders on. And . . ." I fold my hands across my belly protectively and hug it. "I need you to be part of our baby's life. To teach it love and patience and how to stand up to a bully because I'm not always good at that. But most of all, I need you because I've lived without you before and after I fell in love with you, and that life is cold and lonely. It's ugly, and I promise to do better this time. I'll never let you go again."

He breathes a sigh of relief and pulls me against his chest. I hold him tight. It's been so long, too long, since he held me like this.

"I'm not with Ashley. I needed a friend. Someone I could trust to give it to me straight. She happened to be in town and we had lunch and talked. About you. That's all." He pulls back to look in my eyes. "As far as the baby, of course I want it. I want it all with you, Amber. I want a house, a family and a happily ever after."

"Did I miss something? Did you just propose?" Logan asks walking in with a tray full of food.

"No way, man. I wouldn't do that without asking your permission first."

"Really? Then what's going on?"

Mason and I look at each other.

"It's your call," Mason says.

"No. It's ours."

Logan puts the tray on the rolling table. Before we have the opportunity to get into the details of what he walked in on, a technician comes in with an ultrasound machine. My son looks scared.

"What is that? What's it for?"

I jump in before anyone else can answer. "It's fine, Logan. They just need to take a look at something. Can you do me a favor and give us a few minutes. Please."

"Okay. Do you mind if I take the fries?"

"Help yourself."

"You coming, Mr. Archer?"

Mason looks at me for help. I don't want him to leave. Just like I said a few minutes ago, I want him by my side as my partner. I want him to enjoy every part of this experience.

"Actually, honey, I'd really like for Mason to stay here with me."

"Okay." Logan says and walks out.

"If you're not far enough along, we may not be able to see anything." The woman says once I pull my underwear down. She dims the lights, and enters our information into the machine before putting a condom and gel on the wand that goes inside me.

I hold onto Mason's hand as we watch the monitor, waiting to see what it might show.

"Here's the little bugger," she says with a smile. She turns a knob and we hear a swishing, with a definite pattern. "That's the heartbeat," she says. Taking pictures and zooming in and out of different parts of the image.

I pull my eyes from the monitor to glance at Mason. He watches the monitor open mouthed. I squeeze his hand. My heart thrums. We're having a baby. Mason and I are having a baby!

Once the ultra sound is complete, the technician hands us a picture she printed of our little munchkin.

"We're really doing this?" Mason asks, excitement shining in his eyes.

I nod. "We're really doing this!"

"I love you so much," he leans in to kiss me.

Once his lips meet mine I thread my fingers through his hair. Mason slips his arms beneath me and holds me close as he deepens the kiss. He pulls away suddenly, and I'm worried the gravity of the situation might have hit him. We're going to be responsible for a life, a brand new, precious life.

"Don't look so disappointed," Mason says trailing his fingers down the side of my cheek. "You'll have plenty of me once we get you home." He looks up at the IV bag. "But right now, there's a certain teenage boy I need to kiss up to."

"Why's that?"

"Because he's going to hate me when he finds out I knocked his mother up. I better go get his blessing to marry you before we tell him."

I watch Mason walk out of my room. I hate watching him leave. I don't think that will ever change, but I'm okay. This time is different. This time I know he's coming back.

Epilogue

"Since you promised me a brother, and now I have a sister. I think the Mustang should be mine when I pass my driving test." The crowd laughs at the best man's speech. "And don't forget, I gave you permission to marry my mother," Logan says, holding up his glass of ginger ale.

The wedding guests lift their champagne flutes and drink. Seconds later the clinking of silverware against the empty glasses begins.

I give the crowd what they want and kiss my husband.

The reception is small. Close friends and family. Neither side has too many people, although I invited Keith's family, and Mason invited Ashley and her husband. I wasn't too thrilled about that one but I did say the reception is mainly so that he and his family have the experience.

When I was released from the hospital, Mason insisted that he, Logan and I hop on a flight to Vegas to get married. Vegas to make it memorable. The marriage itself was necessary for the medical insurance since Mason's coverage is better and cheaper than mine.

"There's something about your smile," Mason says, during our first dance as husband and wife. "You look like the cat that ate the canary,"

"It's seeing you in that tux, and knowing I get to get to undress you later." I tease.

"You plan on having your way with me, Mrs. Archer?"

"You know it, Mr. Archer."

After the first dance, Keith's mother and sister come speak with us.

"You're baby girl is so precious." Rose says, pulling me into an embrace.

"Thank you," Mason says, with a smile before I can respond.

"If you ever need a babysitter, you know where I am. And I don't mean just Logan. I'd love to look after that little girl."

I feel bad. I know she hoped Keith and I would have had other children. She loves spoiling Logan and her other grandchildren.

"Would you like a moment alone?" Mason asks out of respect for the relationship I still have with my in-laws.

"No." Maggie answers without hesitation. "You should hear this, too."

"We want you to be happy, dear," Rose says. "We've been so worried about you since Keith died. He loved you so much, he would've wanted you to be happy. It's clear that Mason makes you very happy."

"He does." I look up and smile at my husband like a lovesick teenager.

"We just want you to know, Amber, that no matter what happens. You'll always be part of the family. That goes for Mason and little Kaylee too."

"Thank you, Rose." My groom leans down and kisses her cheek. I can tell from the high pitched giggle, that Mason won her over and made her night.

"See, and you worried they would hate you for marrying me," Mason slips his arm around my waist and whispers in my ear as they return to their tables.

"I think it's because Rose is sweet on you."

"Hey, whatever works."

He takes my hand in his and leads us back out to the dance floor.

"Are you happy?" I ask, loosing myself in my husband's beautiful pools of blue.

"More so than I ever thought possible."

This time Ashley interrupts us. "I could attest to that. In all the years I know him put together, I've never seen him smile as much as he has tonight."

"No way!" I protest.

"And he never looked at me the way he looks at you. I saw it, even when he tried to hide it at the pizzeria. I knew he was head over heels in love with you. I'm really happy you guys worked it out." She looks over her shoulder. "Now if you'll excuse me, I need to get back to my husband. With three little ones at home, we don't have a night to ourselves very often."

Her husband waves to Mason, and my handsome husband nods back to him.

"Do you know him well?" I ask.

"Well enough." Mason shrugs. "He was my roommate."

I slap at his chest. "You never told me they got married."

He shrugs with a smile before placing a quick kiss on my lips. "I like it when you're jealous."

"Excuse me." Logan pats Mason on the shoulder. "Would you mind if I have a dance with Mom?"

"Not at all, little man." Mason lets go of me and takes a step back so I can dance with my son. "That was quite a speech," he says from a foot away as Logan and I sway back and forth.

"Thought you'd like it. Especially the part about giving me the Mustang."

"You got me dude, who would've thought with all the testosterone I have rushing through my veins that we'd have a girl?"

"Please." I roll my eyes. "You wish. Besides, I think you're getting ahead of yourselves."

"Ahead of ourselves? She's already here. I just thought when they couldn't tell what the sex was that it was a boy."

"That was reason enough to suspect she was a girl. If it was a boy, just like the rest of the male species, he'd be happy to show off his thing."

"Oh, God, Mom." Logan lets go of me. "Don't start talking about my thing, and especially not about Mason's thing."

I shake my head. And look at my husband who's frozen in place, staring at me.

"I know I don't even have my permit yet. But you say all the time how the years go by so fast."

"They do. And you never know what surprises come along the way."

"Wait, wait, wait." Mason puts his hand up. "I think your mother is trying to tell us something."

I offer a small, guilty smile.

Mason narrows his blue eyes on me, "Are you saying you're—"

"Pregnant."

"Eww, Mom, really? Do you two have to go at it like rabbits?" Logan asks looking like I just vomited all over him. Logan shivers, "I need to get some air and get the image of you two out of my head."

"You're pregnant?" Mason asks in disbelief.

I nod with an ear to ear smile. "I've been dying to tell you all day. I wanted this to be a surprise."

"Are you sure?" He asks, pulling me against his body.

"I haven't gone to the doctor yet, but the test came back positive and I'm feeling pretty sick.

Mason's eyes shine as he lifts me up and slides me down his body. "We're having a baby?" He says once my feet hit the ground. "Another baby?"

"Yes!" I nod, excitement running like a drug through my veins.

"Hey everybody," Mason yells to our guests, holding me close to his side. "I knocked her up again!"

The crowd cheers, the glasses clink, and I know I found my happily ever after.

Thank you for reading Beyond Gray Skies. I hope you enjoyed it! If you did, please tell a friend and post a review on the site that you bought it from.

Sneak Peak of Regret Me Not

For Mackenzie Green life is full of regrets; regrets from choices she made in the past, regrets for the things she'll never see in her future. She regrets letting her grades slip while her sister was in rehab, ensuring she'll never break away from the rumor-run, small town she lives in. She regrets breaking up with her future All American football playing boyfriend, Brayden Turner out of fear of getting hurt. Most of all she regrets every decision she made leading up to the night that changed her life forever.

It's only after Brayden cuts her off completely that Mackenzie realizes how much she wants him in her life. She's learns that losing what you love breaks you, but sometimes it's the only way to tap into your inner strength.

Can Mackenzie find the courage to learn from her mistakes and move forward or will she spend her days consumed with regrets?

Chapter 1
The Homecoming Dance

Brayden looks at me with the same intense longing I've seen in his eyes all night. Every touch lasts a moment too long, making me want to taste the sweet warmth of his delicious lips. Every look smolders, bringing color to my cheeks, as he pairs a look with a stroke of my exposed skin.

His hand moves from the top of my back, slowly, straight down to the bottom, pressing me against him, making my body tingle, my insides quiver. He knows what he's doing, that he's creating a fierce desire inside me; that's what he's counting on.

He inches in a bit closer as we move in perfect precision to the music, slow music that seems to want to keep us on the dance floor, locked in each other's arms.

Holding me close, he brushes up against me. In an attempt to escape the look in his soft brown eyes I lean into his chest, and rest my head there, bringing me right up against the warmth of his body. The familiar smell of his cologne comforts me, but only for a moment before it feeds the growing fire burning deep inside.

I want him.

Each beat of my heart, every breath, brings me closer to succumbing to this unyielding desire. Every sweet caress serves to convince me we belong together. No matter how I try to convince myself that it's wrong, that we'll only end up hurting each other in the long run, I keep getting lost in the pleasure the present promises.

A soft moan passes his lips, and I hold him tighter, my fingers dig into the hard muscles beneath his clothes. I know I don't have the strength to fight the cataclysmic pull that keeps me drawn to him, that keeps me unable to move out of his arms.

I look around the large, dimly lit room, but only for a few seconds. I don't care about anything else in here, not the decorations hung on the walls, or the bubble machine chugging away on the side. I don't care to see what the other girls are wearing, or even if they're pretty. Not tonight.

The only thing I want, the only thing my brain can wrap itself around is Brayden; Brayden's brown eyes and award winning smile. The feel of his arms holding me against him. The fresh clean smell that hangs on him no matter the time of day or night.

All I know is Brayden.

"I miss you," he whispers, his breath tickling my ear. "I'm so glad you're here."

I give myself the benefit of the doubt, thinking I could chance a look in his eyes and not be captivated by their intensity.

I'm wrong. There's heat in his eyes. They're smoldering.

Unconsciously I lick my lip before answering. "I miss you, too."

He takes a chance. I knew he would eventually. He leans in, and presses his lips against mine. They're soft and warm, as always. I don't pull away, I want more. My mouth opens, inviting him in as my hips press against his.

I want this kiss. I've wanted it since Brayden picked me up. I didn't initiate it because I wasn't sure one kiss would satiate me. I'm not sure one night will either.

His eyes trail from my head, down, all the way down. I don't miss how they hesitate at the neckline of my dress. I know he wants to bring his hands there; they always seemed to gravitate to that area. But Brayden, being the perfect gentleman, resists the urge. It's a battle apparent in his eyes. He waits and feels me out. He can read my reactions. He knows my body, just as well as he knows my heart.

"Do you feel that?" He brings his mouth beside my ear and speaks in a soft, velvety tone. "Your pulse racing? The swirling of your stomach? Do you feel the heat between us?

It's a wild fire burning out of control. It's getting bigger and hotter by the minute."

He kisses me again. This time there's hunger and need in his kiss. One hand gets lost in my hair, the fingers on the other hand press into my flesh. He wants more. He wants all of me, and I want to give it. Give in. I swallow hard, still delusional that I have an ounce of control over what I'm doing or where things are leading.

"Kenzie, I love you. And I want you back."

That's the final straw. It's the reason I came. I want to make sure it's still there. Not just the attraction that never left, but the love, the desire, the all-out need for each other. I've felt it all night. I see it every time he looks at me. But hearing his declaration, I'm lost, prisoner to his every whim.

Also by Danielle Sibarium

The Eternity Series
For Always (Eternity 1)
And Forever (Eternity 2)

The Heart Waves Series
Heart Waves (1)
Breaking Waves (2)
Waves of Love (3)
Heart Waves Series Boxed Set

Man Up
Each book revolves around a different couple, and each
book has its own HEA
Man Up Party Boy (Noah and Lexi)
Man Up Playboy (Cooper and Selene)
Man Up Husband (Troy and Marlena)
Man Up Step Brother (Jagger and Allie) (Free on KDP)
*Man Up Soldier (Jagger and Allie without the step brother
element)*

Stand Alones
To My Hero: A Blog of Our Journey Together
Into You
Regret Me Not
My Russian Nightmare
Broken Pieces
Beyond Gray Skies
Coming in 2022 Sliding Home

Acknowledgements

To you, the person that took a chance on this book. Thank you. Thank you for sharing a piece of your life with me and allowing me to share a slice of my imagination with you. It's been an incredible ride, and I appreciate the company.

Thank you to my my husband Alex who always supports and encourages me to keep pushing forward and focused on the future. Thank you to my children who are finally old enough to look at and help with my social media.

Thank you to my beta readers. You guys are the best. You'll never know how much you mean to me. I appreciate your enthusiasm to read and give your honest feedback. My characters are well-rounded and my books better because of you.

Thank you to Lainey Da Silva, friend and PA. I am so happy to be working with you.

Thank you Clarise Tan from CT Cover Creations for creating a beautiful cover. It's a pleasure, as always, working with you. This is one of my favorite parts of the process.

Thank you once again to the Jackson Writer's Group. I have grown so much as a writer since I walked into my first meeting. You guys are the best! Even though members have come and gone over the years, I have always felt encouraged and supported. RIP Karen Riley and Larry Meegan you will always be remembered, appreciated and thought of fondly.

About the Author

Danielle is a romance author best known for steamy romances that make you laugh and cry as her characters come of age and grow emotionally.

Danielle grew up as an only child of divorced parents in Brooklyn, New York. Her imagination was developed at an early age. Surrounded by stuffed animals and imaginary friends, she transported herself into a fantasy world full of magic and wonder. Books were the gateway between her play world and reality.

Danielle always loved dialogue and in elementary school began writing plays and short stories. This is when she began to understand she could not only bring her fantastical world to life for herself, but she could enchant others as well.

In 2007 Danielle collaborated with Charlotte Doreen Small to write songs for her CD *More*. Danielle wrote the lyrics for *Take My Hand*, and *Goodbye*, while Charlotte contributed the melody. In 2011 her Debut novel For Always topped Amazon charts in the Young Adult category.

Danielle graduated from Fairleigh Dickinson University with honors, and currently lives in North Carolina with her husband, three children and their family dog.